Zerocuse.

Billy Mungovan.

outskirts
press

Outskirts Press, Inc.
http://www.outskirtspress.com

Paperback ISBN: 978-1-9772-2995-3

Outskirts Press and the "OP" logo are trademarks belonging to Outskirts Press, Inc.

PRINTED IN THE UNITED STATES OF AMERICA

To Grady & Miles. I love you more than you'll ever know.
Or maybe you do know, in which case I've done my job correctly.

"A human being is a part of a whole, called by us Universe, a part limited in time and space. He experiences himself, his thoughts and feelings as something separated from the rest, a kind of optical delusion of his consciousness. The striving to free oneself from this delusion is the one issue of true religion. Not to nourish it but to try to overcome it is the way to reach the attainable measure of peace of mind."
—Albert Einstein

"I thought that I was free but I'm just one more prisoner of time, alone within the boundaries of my mind."
—Jackson Browne

Tennessee Valley Trail
Mill Valley, CA

Jenny and I are watching the boys ahead of us, making sure they are dutifully stopping at each trailhead as instructed while the four of us hike toward the Pacific. The wheels of Charlie's bike roll over the hill in front of us and out of view while little Teddy's shadow runs behind him like a drunken toddler. We get to the beach and Jenny sets up the picnic while I pull out a miniature soccer ball and the three of us boys begin kicking it around. We don't bother setting up goals, instead opting for a sort of Kill The Carrier–type game where Charlie and Teddy try to tackle me as I dribble around in nonsensical figure eights. After the sun sets but before it's dark, we tread back to the car and pack everything up and eventually drive back to the house and get in our jammies and brush our teeth and go to bed—the four of us in our beautiful bubble.

Part I

Friday

CHAPTER 1

I was the first to board. I handed the flight attendant my jacket and ordered a glass of red wine and sat down in seat 2B. The flight attendant said nothing and went right to work and hung up the jacket and brought me the wine. Thank you, Delta. The pangs hit my gut right after I took my seat, but the wine helped. I woke up in the air, my empty wine glass cleared. The flight attendant returned and I ordered another.

We landed and I got off the plane at Hancock International Airport in my old hometown, and the airport ceiling felt low. There seemed to be nobody around. I was listening to "Trouble in Mind" by Nina Simone, which in retrospect was probably a little on the nose. There was a Sbarro pizza window open next to a Syracuse University–themed sports bar with nobody in either—not even any workers. I spotted a young family sitting in front of an empty gate. It was unclear if they were coming or going. I made my way out past security, where my mother was waiting for me in the same jacket and scarf she seemed to have worn since childhood.

"There he is! How was the flight, Mr. First Class?"

"Good," I said. "Great to see you, Mom." We hugged.

"Oh good," she said. "Dad and I are really excited to have you home. It should be a fun weekend. I can't believe it's been 20 years since you first left."

"Yep."

We weren't even to the car when she brought it up.

"Have you talked to Jenny lately? You can't just ignore her forever."

"Mom, let's not do this right now. I'm tired."

"Why not? She's your wife, for God's sake."

"I'm not ignoring her. She doesn't want to speak to me. She wants space so I'm giving her space."

"She doesn't want space. She needs you, honey. She's all alone out there in that house and you're wandering around New York City all by yourself. You must need her too."

"I don't have a choice, Mom. She doesn't want to see me. That's all I know."

"Look, it was tragic. I pray for you both every day. But that doesn't mean you two can't work this out together. She doesn't still blame you for it. I'm sure of it."

"I'm not doing this right now."

"C'mon, honey, I'm just trying to help. You two need each other."

"If you don't stop I'm turning around right now and going back to New York. I'm serious. Jesus fucking Christ."

She didn't respond and we had three merciful minutes of silence before we got into the car and drove off.

"You know, you really shouldn't use the Lord's name in vain," she said.

When I got the notification that my 20-year high school reunion was happening, I figured I might as well go. As far as I could tell, nobody there would know about my situation and I needed a break from myself. It might be fun to see what happened to everybody. I figured most of them grew up to be middle-class Republicans, dutifully voting against their own economic interests while fighting the good fight against Obama, socialism, and homos, but who knows? Maybe they would surprise me. It was worth a shot.

After a ridiculous hour of being patronized by my folks, I took the keys to my mom's Chrysler LeBaron and left to grab beers and head over to my old buddy Hogan's house. I hadn't seen him in ages. At the mini-mart I ran into somebody from high school—no clue what her name was. We were Facebook friends and I definitely recognized her; I think we were in 10th-grade health class together and she was on the high school party circuit like everyone else. Kathy? Karen? I felt bad for not remembering. She's white and in high school she was into black dudes, which was rare enough in the '90s to be memorable (probably still is). As soon as she saw me she came over and gave me a hug.

"Jimmy! Wow. I haven't seen you in forever! How are you? Are you okay? Oh shit. I shouldn't ask that. I'm so sorry."

So much for a break.

"No worries. I'm fine. Are you going to the reunion?"

"Of course!" she said. "I'm on the planning committee, silly! We're all so excited so many people are coming in from out of town. Like you! Are you excited?"

"Totally. It's gonna be great to see everybody. Is there an after-party?"

"Of course! It's at John and Katie's house." No clue who they were. "It'll be just like the ragers we used to have in high school. Can't wait!"

"Awesome. See you tomorrow."

"Yay!" She hugged me again.

And that was that. I was back. I bought some Molson Goldens and headed to Hogan's.

CHAPTER 2

I rifled through four therapists and two grief groups in six months after arriving in New York. The low point was the dream therapy group. What a fucking racket. We sat around and discussed our dreams and tried to figure out what they meant. I've always found other people's dreams insanely tedious (I thought everybody did), but at the time I was willing to try anything. This group took the cake. We'd spend hour after hour listening to abstract fragments about being chased in the woods or being naked or being scared to have sex or whatever it was, and pretty much every dream came down to the dreamer's insecurities. One day I told a 65-year-old man named Sam to get over his goddamn insecurities already. "You're a grown man, Sam, and you're a huge fucking pussy! You're 65, Sam. Do you wanna die a pussy?" I was asked to leave and that was the end of that.

I did find some solace in the anonymity of New York. Everybody on the street had somewhere to be; nobody wanted anything from me. My job in San Francisco gave me as much time as I needed to deal, but after a month I was ready to get back at it so I told them I needed to move to New York and they obliged. I design software for a living. There's not much more to say about my work.

One thing about having a horrible thing happen to you is it makes everybody around you both extremely accommodating and totally scarce. People around you just kind of disappear—a situation that is significantly amplified in the workplace. Nobody wanted to talk about it in the office and I was happy to let them not talk about it. But I still felt I needed to get the hell out of San Francisco, completely away from the life we'd been living, and start over someplace else. I've always loved New York and I figured it was big enough to swallow me up. Plus the big software conglomerate I work for has a huge office there so it was easy enough to pick up and move, and Jenny wanted nothing to do with me so I left.

New York became its own form of therapy. I wanted to learn everything about it—where everything was, the best routes around town, the best places to eat, the best places to find peace and quiet. I began wandering around by myself after work and on weekends, meandering from neighborhood to neighborhood, bar to bar, restaurant to restaurant. I learned how to maneuver in New York, how to be totally alone while surrounded by millions. I was probably drinking too much but I got into a groove and things started to feel better. I was both "the king of my own skull-sized kingdom" (see: "This is Water" by David Foster Wallace) and part of the wider, functioning world. I met no women and had no interest in them. I wanted to be alone and I was for a full year. For the most part, New York did what it was supposed to do. It swallowed me up.

CHAPTER 3

I knocked on Hogan's door while opening it and walked in. "Dude. Stop beating off," I said.

Hogan appeared from around a corner and gave me a huge hug.

"So good to see you, my brother. Great to have you back in the Cuse."

"Good to see you too, man. I gotta tell you, it's weird being back here. Everything's exactly as I remember it. It's like nothing's changed."

He laughed. "I guess. Come in, come in."

We walked into his small bachelor pad living room with a Navajo rug, framed pictures of Jerry Garcia and Neil Young on the wall, couches around a TV, and a lone crucifix on the mantel. I set the 6-pack onto the coffee table and pulled out two beers.

"I don't drink anymore, dude," Hogan said.

"What? Why not? Mormon? Muslim? Alcoholic?"

"Alcoholic. I can't believe you don't know that. Shit got dark for me after Jessica dumped me. It was bad for a couple of years there."

"No pot, either? You were the king of pot in high school."

"Nope," Hogan said.

"Well fuck, dude. I'm sorry. I suck for not knowing that. I guess we really lost touch for a bunch of years there."

"I know. That was my fault as much as yours. I just wanted to be alone ..."

"I know the feeling."

"... and then my dad died and just made it all worse. But I'm good now. Sober and mellow."

"And into God too, huh?" I said and nodded at the crucifix.

"Yeah, that's helped me a lot, actually. Anyway, what the hell have you been up to?"

It occurred to me that Hogan might not know about my sitch. He hadn't come to the funeral in California. I didn't feel like talking about it.

"Not much. Just working a bunch, wandering around New York. My marriage is pretty much dead but other than that, same old shit. Just taking it one day at a time."

"That's all you can do, my brother. Especially after that horrible shit you went through."

Of course he knew. My mom, small town, one of my oldest friends whom I somehow lost touch with, etc., etc.

"Yeah. I kind of figured people around here wouldn't know about it but I just ran into ... what's her name ... you know, the chick who was into black dudes? I haven't seen her since graduation and she knew about it. Oh well."

"Oh yeah. Katie D'Angelo. I mean, people around here probably know but it's not a big deal. I mean, it's a big deal but nobody's gonna wanna talk about it so you'll be okay."

Good old Hogan.

"Good," I said. "So what's the plan? Are people going out tonight?"

"Yeah, everybody's meeting at The Bitter End. Do you remember Rock?"

"Of course. His dad was our Pop Warner football coach."

"Totally. He bought it a couple of years ago so that's where the old Thomas Jefferson High folks go nowadays. It's where all of those North Side Italians used to go in high school."

"While we were at Grateful Dead Night up at Syracuse University."

"Yup. Let me grab my shit and we'll head over there."

Hogan already had on some tunes and I leaned back into the couch and drank my beer while the sun went down and he got ready for the night. "*If you get confused, listen to the music play,*" the song said. Indeed. I closed my eyes and waited. The sun went down and out we went. Hogan driving, me drinking.

When we walked into The Bitter End there was a crowd of people playing shuffleboard, a TV showing *Goodfellas* on mute, and a jukebox blasting Journey. It was almost full. Everywhere I looked I saw familiar faces whose names I couldn't remember. I weaved my way to the bar where Rock was standing. The lord of the manor.

"Jimmy! What's up, bro?"

He held out his hand and we fist-bumped. Johnny Rock. That's his real name. We were friends as kids and played Pop Warner football together, but we ended up in slightly different but overlapping circles in high school. I always liked him.

"Not much, man. Just back in town for the big reunion. You own this place now? It's great."

"Yeah, it's been great. I love it, mixing it up with everybody. It's a big piece of Syracuse history, you know? What can I get you?"

I ordered a gin and tonic for myself and a Coke for Hogan. I paid up, bid old Johnny Rock farewell, and was turning back toward Hogan when I saw her. Nerves pinched at first, then a sort of calming chemistry cocktail released into the bloodstream. Breathe. This is good. It was not a "dreeeeam weaver!" moment but she represented something important to me. My adolescence, I guess. A time before real life began. It all happened in a second. She was staring at me from ten feet away with those trademark big brown eyes and a big smile. Kelly Donnatelli. The girl with the rhyming name. My first girlfriend. I walked right over to her still holding both drinks and stood there, not knowing if I should go in for the hug.

"Aren't you gonna hug me? C'mon, shy boy!" She laughed and wrapped her arms around my neck and pulled me in. I held out the drinks and hugged her with my elbows. I guess I knew I'd see her but I hadn't thought about it, not even once (not consciously anyway) since deciding to come home. In the moment I realized I hadn't been this close to a woman in what felt like years. She smelled delicious.

"How are you? I was hoping you'd come," she said.

"I almost didn't, but things have been so fucked up for me lately I figured I'd try something new." Her smile disappeared.

I don't know why I said it. I'm not that honest with anybody, much less the 9th-grade girlfriend I hadn't seen in decades.

"Oh no, I'm so sorry," she said. She hugged me again. It was unclear if she knew about my situation. Probably.

"No, I'm sorry. I shouldn't have launched into it in the first five seconds of seeing you again." Change the subject. "So do you still live here? Do you have a family? Kids?"

"I do. I figured you'd know that from Facebook."

Yeah right. Before, I was genuinely interested in other people's lives. I was a regular contributor to Facebook with witty observations and funny pictures of the boys. After, I couldn't deal with it and shut it down.

"Sorry. I've been a little out of touch lately. It's great to see you. You look exactly as I remember you. Are you still in Syracuse?"

"No, I live in Ithaca now. Married, two kids. You know, standard stuff. Life is good, you know?"

"Nice. You got out too."

"Out?"

I changed the subject again—a special skill of mine, by the way. It's something you become good at when you constantly say awkward things to people. We started chatting and I sipped my gin and tonic and Hogan made his way over. We talked about partying at "The Hill" behind the high school, about the time Paulie Malone shotgunned a huge Foster's can and puked all over Lonnie Sawyer while they were making out, and the petty dramas in that summer between 9th and 10th grade when we broke up and started dating other people and how it seemed like the world was going to end from heartbreak but somehow we managed to find the strength to carry on. We laughed at how important it had all seemed, and I suppose it was important in its own way. Being "home" seemed to be working.

After a while, Kelly Donnatelli was whisked away by her old friend Tina, and Hogan and I found a stand-up table by the window and posted up there. The faces streamed past and I wondered if they were happier than I'd been before the accident.

I always thought I had it nailed. A cool job in San Francisco. A house in Mill Valley. A beautiful family. Freedom in the form of security. But these people seemed happy in a different, more genuine way. They lifted each other up off the ground when they hugged and they did shot after shot and actually laughed out loud. They seemed unselfconscious.

But I wasn't really there. The entire time we'd been there we'd heard only '80s songs. "Twilight Zone" by Golden Earring was blaring. It struck me as dark. I looked out the window and decided to sneak out early and head back to my parents' place.

And then, "Jimmy!" Peter Dantonio. My best friend in elementary school—though, to be fair, Peter was everybody's best friend in elementary school. A skateboarder turned prep turned jock turned womanizer (and rumored date rapist) turned sometime coke dealer, all before 12th grade.

"Peter fuckin' Dantonio," I said. "Wow."

We did the bro hug thing: high five at chest level, clasped hands into cross-arms to the chest with a light back tap.

"I've been wondering about you," he said. "You're a friggin' rich guy now, right? Am I right? So good to see you, bro!"

"You still banging Tina over there?"

Peter Dantonio dated Kelly's friend Tina in 9th grade, the same year I dated Kelly Donnatelli. At one point I saw him throw Tina into a wall where a picture frame fell onto her head and the glass broke. They always made up.

"That ho? C'mon, man," Peter said. "I'm married now. Wife, kids, the whole thing."

"So you married Tina?"

"Fuck you!" he said and put me in a headlock.

"Great to see you, dude. You still in the Cuse?"

"Yeah man, living the dream," he said. "So I hear you're in New York now. How's that? Great fuckin' city, right?"

"Yeah, I love the pace."

The small talk was good. It covered all that needed to be said. The distinctive whiff of pot wisped through The Bitter End.

"Somebody's rippin' a J in here? Fuck it, then," Peter said and reached into his jacket pocket and pulled out a machine-rolled joint—a perfect cylinder. He lit it, took a big hit, exhaled toward the ceiling, and extended it to me.

"No thanks, man," I said. "I'm good."

"C'mon, bro. It's a party night!"

"Can't do it. If I smoke that I'm out for the count."

The truth is I haven't been able to smoke pot since the accident. It gives me anxiety and my serotonin levels tank. The depression worsens.

"Suit yourself," he said and passed it to a familiar face next to him, a guy on our high school lacrosse team; he played defense but didn't start—another name I couldn't place.

As I looked around I again noticed everybody in there

was having a great time. Red eyes, loud belly laughs, hugs everywhere. Several people were playing air guitar to "Sweet Child of Mine," and over by the corner a group of guys I sort of recognized (maybe the baseball team guys? soccer team guys?) were standing in a circle screaming the lyrics. Behind the bar Rock poured a long line of tequila shots, maybe twenty in a row, and hands reached in from every direction to grab them. A loud "Cheers!" and down went the shots and a huge roar of hoots and hollers clashed with the loud music, and, for that moment at least, I was totally and completely present. I decided to stay.

CHAPTER 4

Jenny and I met in college and both moved to San Francisco a few months after graduation. We started dating almost immediately and it was great right from the beginning. We agreed not to say "I love you" too early as we both had in previous relationships and we took it slow, which is to say we hung out all of the time, every day, and didn't worry about the future. We didn't discuss marriage or kids. We didn't care that we had no real skills and no plan for life. We were 23. Then 24. 25. And so on. We were still on the college party schedule where weekends started on Thursday and we found a bar in the Mission where they served martinis in pint glasses and we were young enough to make it to those mindless jobs on Fridays completely hung over. Life was easy. Fun.

Jenny was (is) beautiful. She's sweet and funny and smart and all of the wonderful things the best women are. It was never clear why she settled on me—picked me, really—but she did. All in all, a win for me. Maybe for her too, but I never thought so. And that's not just false modesty; I truly am an idiot. Lost. Perpetually homesick.

Lately I've been thinking back on the best parts of my life—preteen skateboarding, late-teen psychedelics experimentation at Grateful Dead shows, those early years in San Francisco with Jenny. I've been trying to remember if life was really better then or if it just seems so in retrospect.

I used to spend my lunch breaks from my mailroom starter job walking around the San Francisco docks near my office, just letting my mind reel. Every night before bed I would read to help me fall asleep, but before I picked up the book I would just stare at the ceiling while my brain processed whatever was going on inside it. I suspect this is the same for most people, but maybe not. I don't know. From therapist #3 in New York I was told I had a minor case of hypomania—a condition which was useful for most of my life but now requires treatment. Before the accident I always had ideas flowing through my mind, lots of energy, a killer sex drive. I could drink and do drugs like a champion and I was generally a buoyant, happy guy. It was essentially a very minor case of bipolar disorder but without the depression. After, its darker cousin arrived: full-on, fuck-me depression.

In New York City I began self-medicating with alcohol, alone, and spent a lot of my time thinking, thinking, thinking about the past.

CHAPTER 5

Later at The Bitter End I wound up talking to my old high school lacrosse teammates, the twin brothers Sean and Michael O'Brien. Two happy Irish guys in a sea of Italians. Sean was an All American and the best player on our high school team. He went on to win a national championship with Syracuse University in 1993, one of the best lacrosse programs in the country back then (and now).

"So are you guys both living in Syracuse?"

"Yeah, we're both still in Eastwood, not far from where we grew up. Our mom is still in that same house," Sean said.

"No shit. I remember your dad. He came to every game."

"So did your mom," said Sean. "She was a maniac in the stands."

"Tell me about it. Back then it really embarrassed me but I'm sure I'd be the same way if I was at my kids' games." Why did I just say that? Move on.

"Wait, I have an idea," said Michael. "Do you wanna fire some shots at a cage tonight? Just like old times."

"Seriously?" I asked.

"Yeah, man. Let's go to the TJ field. It's spring. The cages are set up for the season and I have a bunch of sticks and balls in my trunk. Plus, we're the coaches. Nobody's gonna say anything to us. Hey Z, you wanna get in the cage tonight?"

Z was Zack Aristo, our high school goalie. I noticed he was still in great shape; they all were. Zack started laughing and nodded.

"I've got my goalie shit in my trunk," Z said. "Let's do it."

"Are all of you guys still playing?" I asked.

"Hell yeah! We're in an over-30 league. It's such a blast," Sean said. "We're in first place right now."

I couldn't decide if these guys were pathetic for never progressing past high school or if they had progressed and simply chose to stay in the same neighborhood they'd lived in all their lives and do the things they loved most. Or maybe "progressing" was a bullshit myth; maybe we just are who we are. Wouldn't I rather be on tour with the Dead than thinking about software at my desk all day? Maybe they had it right.

"Let's do it!" said Michael, and the five of us filed out of the bar and hopped into our cars. Hogan never played lacrosse but he was my best friend in Syracuse—one of my oldest friends, in fact—and I planned to keep him by my side the entire weekend.

As we drove off I realized the houses around The Bitter End were more run-down than I remembered growing up. Several were empty with no doors or windows on them. More than one had graffiti on it. Either I didn't notice the squalor as much when I was young or this part of Syracuse was falling apart. Who am I kidding? I thought. These guys are fucking pathetic. I can't even fathom what life would be like in my old neighborhood, and beyond that I can't imagine not having the desire to live in other places and meet people from other places. That's what makes life exciting. Hogan being the exception, although at least he moved to Portland for a bunch of years. Syracuse was a shithole, I thought.

We drove a few short miles to the old high school football/soccer/lacrosse field. The stadium lights were out, so the guys pulled right onto the field and parked along the sidelines facing the field and left their headlights on. In addition to his lax equipment, Z had a twelve-pack in his trunk, and he tossed it to me to carry out to the field.

"Let's run the fast break drill," Sean said. As soon as he said it I remembered how it worked. It's a drill where you have one more offensive player than defensive—4 on 3—and you have to pass the ball quickly to create an open man who takes the shot. Hogan never played, but he was generally athletic and sober so he was our fourth man against the imaginary defense. We were set up in a square around the goal, and on the first try we passed the ball perfectly and I took the open shot and scored.

"Too slow, Z!" Sean said.

"Fuck off. There's no defense and it's dark out here. Run it again."

We ran it again and Z made a great save on a shot from Sean.

"Boom!" Z said and zipped the ball back at Sean's head. Sean was the All American and easily moved aside and caught it. These guys were still really good.

We ran it about ten more times and then sat around the goal and opened beers in the glow of the car headlights.

"So Jimmy. How do you like Manhattan? Expensive, isn't it?" Sean said.

"Yeah, but it's worth it. I like the pace."

"It's crazy there. We went down a few years ago for a Yankee playoff game. It was too crazy. And, man, expensive."

"What do you guys do for a living?" I asked.

"Mikey and I are both teachers at the high school. I teach history," Sean said.

"I teach 9th-grade Earth Science," Michael said.

"Yeah, it's a good gig. Plus we coach the lax team, which is fun. Almost made states last year and we're off to a good start this year," Sean said.

"What are the kids like these days?" I said.

"Fuckin' zombies," Sean said. "Always on their phones fucking with each other. There were a lot more fights when we were kids. It was more, like, interactive back then." He said this like it was a good thing. "These kids are all zoned out."

"Yeah, they're pretty horrible to each other, at least in my class," Michael said. "They move in packs and gang up on the kids who aren't like them."

"That's pretty much how it was when we were in high school," Hogan said.

"Exactly," I said. "Do they still fit into '*The Breakfast Club*' mold? Like four or five different cliques who all hate each other?"

"Yeah, I guess so," Michael said. "I never thought about it that way. But yeah, there's all these different groups and they all hate each other. I mean, some of them do well and play sports and will go to college and will probably turn out okay like us. You know, the geeks and the jocks. Most of the kids, though, they don't give a shit."

"What do you mean?" I said.

"They don't give a shit. They don't do any homework, they don't care if they fail, and they basically have no hope to do anything with their lives. Every year I try to save one or two, but most of the kids who don't try are never going anywhere. Some of them are in jail before they even graduate. It sucks."

"Bummer," I said.

"The Syracuse city public school system is fucked," Michael said. "It does the best it can but garbage in, garbage out, you know?"

"That seems a little harsh," I said.

"It's true," Sean said. "Last year a kid brought a gun into school and accidentally shot a girl. It really was an accident but that kid is probably fucked for life."

"Did she live?" I said.

"Yeah, she's okay," Sean said. "But who the fuck brings a gun to school? How does a 15-year-old even have a gun? What the fuck is wrong with these kids? It's like they've given up before they even started."

I finished my beer and crumpled up the can and tossed it at the goal. I opened another.

"What about you?" Michael said.

"What do you mean?"

"What do you do?"

"Software stuff. Nothing special."

"But I hear you make the big bucks, right?"

"I do alright," I said, wanting to change the subject I'd

brought up. "What about you, Z?"

"I run Peppinos. Bought it a few years back," Z said.

"No shit," I said. "I fuckin' love Peppinos pizza. I grew up on it. My mom ordered it every Friday night. They used to cut the pieces into long rectangle strips instead of triangles."

"Still do," he said.

"You guys open right now?"

Z looked at his watch. "We just closed at midnight but we could go in there and make a pizza if you want."

"Oh dude. That'd be amazing," I said. I hadn't eaten since breakfast in Manhattan that morning, which seemed like days ago. I hadn't eaten regularly in a year. "Let's go."

We left the empties on the lacrosse field and headed back to the cars. On the way to Peppinos the pangs started up again.

"I'm really fucked up, dude," I said to Hogan.

"You've had like eight beers since you came to my house. And gin."

"It's not that. I'm not that buzzed. Ridiculous tolerance these days. But I feel like shit inside almost all the time. And it's not getting better."

"Listen, man. You've been through hell."

"I know," I said. "It's just ... I don't know."

"I hear ya," he said. Good old Hogan. "No worries, man. Your song is on. From your first show. Buffalo '89."

He turned up the stereo and we drove the rest of the way without speaking. "*And I say row ... Jimmy row ... gonna get there ... I don't know.*"

As we drove to Peppinos I once again noticed how

run-down the houses were. Then I realized I was looking at the very same graffiti-tagged houses I'd seen earlier. We passed by The Bitter End on the way to Peppinos and I could see in the bar's front window, right where Hogan and I had been standing. The festivities were still in full swing. I looked but didn't see Kelly through the window in the moment we passed by. Almost immediately we pulled up in front of Peppinos, just one block down.

Z unlocked the door, turned on the lights, and pointed at the large refrigerator behind the counter.

"Help yourselves, fellas. I'll fire up the oven."

I grabbed three Labatt's bottles and a Coke for Hogan. Behind the counter I saw two mousetraps, set. We sat at one of the three four-tops while Z went to work. There were a few broken floor tiles beneath the table.

"Jimmy, man. It's been a long time. You too, Hogan," Sean said.

"I know," Hogan said. "I live out in Manlius now. I don't come back to the old neighborhood that often. Ever, really."

"So what do you do out there in Manlius?" Sean said.

"I'm a firefighter."

"No fuckin' way! That's awesome. Firefighters are real heroes," Sean said.

Here we go with the *Fox News* patriotism bullshit, I thought. I sipped my beer and looked out the window.

"A lot of people say that," Hogan said. "Mostly we just sit around. But I like it. Sometimes we get to help people and maybe someday we'll save a life or two."

"I'm serious, man. Nine eleven? That shit was balls to the wall. Where would we be without those guys?"

"I know," Hogan said. "Everybody says that too. For me it's not really about the hero fantasy. It's just a good job working with good guys, trying to be there when people need us. Same as a doctor or a nurse or an ambulance driver. Doctors do a helluva lot more for people than we do on a daily basis, but I always see people wearing FDNY shirts and hardhats at Jets games and it's cool and all, but why not wear like ER scrubs or a stethoscope or something? It's kind of silly to all of us at the station."

"That's crazy, man," Sean said. "Firefighters are cool. Doctors are fuckin' dorks!" Sean, Michael, and Z were laughing hysterically while Hogan just cracked a wry smile—a closed-mouth smile with one side of his mouth turned up. I smiled at that.

Z put a pizza in the oven and came over and sat down. He cracked a beer.

"So how come you guys moved back to the Cuse after college?" I said. "And with you guys"—I pointed at Sean and Z—"how come you never left?"

"I didn't like college," Z said. "I went to Lemoyne for a couple of years but it was boring and too much money and I was basically sick of school. I'd been doing that shit my whole life, you know? So I quit and started tending bar at The Bitter End, way back before Rock bought it. I was picking up chicks left and right. Fucking cleaning up, you know? Best years of my life."

I pictured Wooderson from *Dazed and Confused*.

"I kind of dug college," Sean said.

"I bet," I said. "You won a national championship."

"That was the whole deal for me," Sean said. "That was

my only goal in life and I hit it. But then I realized there's more to life than lacrosse."

Huh.

"So after SU," he said, "I wanted to give back a little and get into teaching and I had some connections at the high school. So ..."

"Plus our dad got sick," Michael said. Michael was the quieter of the two. I'd forgotten that.

"Yeah," Sean said. "So we wanted to be with him and our mom. And look, we love it here. This is our home."

"That makes sense," I said. "But I just couldn't wait to get the fuck out of here. I mean, it's nothing against Syracuse. I would've wanted to leave wherever I grew up. If I grew up in fuckin' Paris I would've wanted to get out."

"Paris sucks," Z said. "Those Frenchie douchebags hate America."

I let that one go.

"I just meant no matter where I grew up I would've wanted to bail. At that age I just wanted to get out and see the world and live someplace new. I still feel that way."

"Me too," Hogan said. "That's why I went to Portland after graduation. I wanted to check out someplace new and De La Rosa was up there. Remember him? He's still there. But then my dad got sick too and I wanted to be with him in his last years. Then I got hired at the station and just kind of stayed."

"Yeah. I like to go on vacations and stuff," Sean said. "But I never wanted to live anyplace else. Everybody I know is here. My whole family. I don't want to be away from my family, you know?"

It made sense, logically speaking, but I wasn't sold. I loved the idea of home and I hadn't really had one since Jenny essentially kicked me out and I moved to New York. I missed it, that sense of place. But why not Syracuse? I loved my childhood. These guys were okay. And yet.

"Yeah," I said. "But still. I just had this urge to get away."

"Get away from what?" Hogan said, that wry smile creeping up again.

"I don't know," I said. "Just get away. Check shit out."

I guess I had no real reason for wanting to leave and these guys had good reasons to stay. A buzzer went off.

"Pizza time, bitches," Z said.

"Let's get it on!" Sean said. "Bring us another round too."

"What am I, your fuckin' mother?"

"Fuck you," Sean said and threw a bottle top at him.

I got up and walked to the fridge while Z walked over to the pizza oven. In less than ten seconds' time he took the pizza out of the oven, laid it on the butcher-block countertop, and sliced it into the Peppinos trademark horizontal strips. He brought it over to the table while I doled out the next round to everybody except Hogan.

As we ate we talked about our old lacrosse team and how that one kid who played defense put a shotgun in his mouth in his bedroom while his parents watched TV downstairs and how we all went to the funeral. We talked about partying at The Hill and about how long ago high school seemed and our old lax coach who rode our asses every day after school and who is now dead. The after-midnight pizza was delicious. It was as if I hadn't eaten in days.

CHAPTER 6

When we were in middle school, Hogan and I went everywhere on our skateboards. We'd meet at this little island—a grass roundabout with a one-way sign that we named "Arrow Circle"—on Sedgwick Drive and would head off to wherever we wanted to go. Hogan lived right around the corner from me; you could get from my house to his on the same sidewalk without crossing a street, though by this age we took pride in riding our skateboards on the street. Street skaters. Some days we would meet at Arrow Circle and skate to the McDonald's at Shop City, a local strip mall, or to our middle school where we'd set up a ramp and would skate off the walls or to anybody's house we wanted to hang out with. We were in that late phase of adolescence, our early teens, where we still played on our skateboards and we were just starting to get interested in girls but weren't yet interested in alcohol or pot.

One Friday night in the summer before our 9th-grade year we skated to Eastwood to check out The Hill where the high school kids partied. It was about four miles from our houses, and we crossed over several major streets and even had to wait at red lights on our boards. The meeting spot was the O'Brien brothers' house.

When we got there a crew of nearly 12 kids was assembled on and around the front steps of the O'Brien home. No parents seemed to be around. Eastwood was right in between two different middle school districts, and while the O'Brien twins went to the same middle school as Hogan and me, there were kids from a neighboring middle school there as well. Kids we didn't know. As we skated up I took an inventory of which kids we knew.

Sean O'Brien was holding court from his top step.

"Here's the deal, people!" he said. "We're heading up to Elmwood Avenue and we'll go up the dead end there. Those are the best steps up to The Hill."

In groups of two or three we filed onto the sidewalk and street and moved as a young teenage mob toward Elmwood Avenue. Hogan and I walked side by side carrying our boards in the middle of the pack.

"Hey," a voice said from behind. A female voice. "You guys know any tricks?"

I turned around and there were two girls smiling at us. At least that's how I remember it.

"We know some tricks," Hogan said. "But we charge to see 'em."

"Aw, come on," the cuter one said. Big brown eyes. Brown hair. Freckles. Boobs. "Show us the coolest trick you can do."

"Ten bucks," Hogan said.

"Okay, ten bucks," she said. The other one was laughing but hadn't chimed in.

Hogan jogged out to the street, laid down his board, and after a few kicks to get some momentum he tried to do a kick-flip. His board under-rotated and landed wheels up while Hogan tripped onto the street. The girls laughed.

"What a gyp!" the cute one said. "I'm not paying ten bucks for that!" She and her friend laughed. I stayed silent on the sidewalk.

"You try," she said, pointing to me.

"No way," I said.

"C'mon," she said, smiling.

"Nope. Not a chance. Why don't you try?" I said, holding out my board.

"Okay. Why not?"

She took the board, which seemed enormous in her small arms, and walked out to the street. She laid it down, put one foot on top, and tried to skate forward. She wobbled and hopped off, running a few steps past the board.

"Whoa!" she said.

"You need some help?" Hogan said.

"Yes," she said. "From him," and pointed to me.

"I'm Jimmy," I said.

"Kelly Donnatelli," she said.

"Huh. Rhyming name."

"I know. My parents are crazy. But I'm over it."

"I like it."

She reached out her hand, palm down, and I realized she didn't want to shake but was holding it out so I could help her balance on the skateboard. I don't think I'd ever held hands with a girl before that. She put one foot on the board again and kicked and I held her hand while she put her second foot on the board and we glided down Elmwood Avenue toward The Hill.

When we got to the bottom of the stone steps leading up to The Hill, I picked up my board and Kelly and I ascended the steps side by side, Hogan and Kelly's friend—whatever her name was—in line behind us. We could hear a boom box with rap music playing further up. As we got closer to the music but before we found its source, police sirens pulled up to the base of the stairs at Elmwood Avenue, lights flashing.

"Cherries and berries!" Hogan yelled.

"Fuck the po-lice!" Peter Dantonio yelled up ahead.

Our mob of middle-schoolers scattered in every direction but down. Kelly, her friend, Hogan, and I ran together horizontally across The Hill through trees and bushes for what seemed like a long time but was likely no more than five minutes. The cops weren't interested in us and we exited the woods two blocks over from Elmwood Avenue.

"This is my street," Kelly said. "That's my house over there."

Less than one year later, I lost my virginity in that house.

CHAPTER 7

We finished off the pizza and our second round of beers and Z did a quick cleanup. He shut down the oven, turned off the lights and locked the door, and we left Peppinos and walked back in the direction of The Bitter End.

"I hear people are headed up to The Hill later on," Sean said while we walked.

"Awesome," I said. "We're in."

Hogan chuckled. "Why not?" he said. "I've had four Cokes. Let's rip it up!"

When we arrived we opened the door to The Bitter End and "Girls" by The Beastie Boys was blaring. Sean, Michael, and Z were headed toward the bar while Hogan and I hung back by the door, silently parting ways with my old lax buddies in the way guys do.

I looked around and was relieved to see Kelly talking to Tina in the corner, just the two of them. She looked up and presumably noticed I was back, to the extent that she was thinking about me at all. She smiled and turned back to Tina.

"I'm getting a cocktail, dude. Another Coke?"

"No way," Hogan said. "I'm wired."

I made eye contact with Kelly on my way back from the bar and she smiled and flashed me a peace sign. In the moment I couldn't recall the last time somebody had flashed me a peace sign. Years, at a minimum.

A few minutes later she made her way over to us.

"Here she is," I said. "The girl with the rhyming name."

"Tina's driving me insane. She's so boring. Nobody cares about your lazy husband, amiright?"

"Is she unhappy?"

"Who knows? She's just fishing for sympathy."

"Women do that," Hogan said.

"I know," Kelly said. "But you're supposed to give it to them, Hogan. Is that why you're still single?"

"Wait, don't turn this around on ..."

She cut him off. "Why are you still single, anyway?"

"Yeah, why are you?" I said.

"I just haven't met anybody since Jessica dumped me."

"It's okay to be gay, nowadays," I said. "Even in Syracuse."

"Fuck off. Syracuse isn't exactly crawling with 30-year-old single ladies."

"You're 38," I said.

"Well," he said.

Kelly laughed and gave Hogan a kiss on the cheek. "You're a good one, Hogan. You'll find somebody. Or somebody will find you."

"In my experience," I said, "that's usually the way it works. They find you."

"Is that how you remember us?" Kelly said.

"Yup."

"Huh. I seem to recall you staring at me all day in 9th

grade Earth Science. Every time I looked up you were looking at me."

"No way," I said. "You wish."

"You did! You were constantly trying to make eyes with me."

"I don't remember that. All I remember with any amount of clarity is the night we met when we ran from the cops on The Hill and the first time we did it. Everything else is just memory noise."

"Memory noise. Please. You don't remember our first kiss?"

"Under the lights outside The Palace Theater. *Dirty Dancing*. First snow of the year."

"See? That wasn't memory noise, was it?"

Hogan began singing, *"I had the time of my life."*

"The girlfriend I had after you," I said.

"Tammy Nigello."

"She never let me live that one down. I don't know why I told her about it. No girl ever wants to believe their boyfriend ever had a romantic moment in their life before them."

"Guys are that way too," she said. "They're actually worse about it. My husband's still jealous of you for taking my virginity."

"Really?"

"Really. He brought it up before I came here this weekend. Told me not to lose it again."

"That's why they call it losing your virginity. Can't be found again and certainly can't be lost twice."

She smiled and pointed at the speaker where "Sister Christian" was blaring.

"How funny is that?" she said.

"This is the best part," Hogan said, and then yelled, "*Motorin'!*"

Peter Dantonio strolled up. Still tall and burly, ever the high school football captain albeit now a drunk and stoned one. He grabbed Hogan by the neck and started belting out the song with him. "*What's your price for flight?*" they yelled and wandered off a few feet away and kept singing. Hogan wasn't drunk but had no problem blending in. Such a good dude.

"Do you wanna go outside and get some air?" she said.

"You read my mind."

"I do that."

We walked outside and away from the few people smoking by the door.

"Buzzards," I said. "We used to call them 'buzzards,' right?"

"Oh my God. I haven't thought about that in years. The smoking heavy-metal kids with the long feathered hair and Metallica and Led Zeppelin patches on their jean jackets."

"Always playing Hacky Sack," I said.

"Yes!"

We both watched a police car as it rolled past. Kelly waved.

"So how are you?" she said.

"What do you mean?"

"Just, how are you?"

"I'm good. What about you? Are you happy?"

"You're always wondering if people are happy. Yes, I'm happy, Jimmy. What is it with you and the happy thing?"

"I don't know. It's just, this whole night I've been trying to figure out if all of these people are really happy. I think they are."

"These people?" she said.

"You know, Syracuse people."

"Aren't you Syracuse people?"

"I mean, technically. But you know what I mean."

"No, I don't," she said.

"Wait, I'm sorry. I didn't mean to offend you. I'll shut up."

"Jimmy, I'm not offended at all. I'm just trying to figure out why you think you're different from 'these people.'"

"I don't. I mean, I don't know. Maybe you're right. I've always felt distanced from Syracuse. Even when I was in high school. I never felt like I belonged here."

"Oh, please. You were a popular lacrosse player who always had girlfriends. You were at every party and everybody liked you. Gimme a break, Jimmy."

"What are you talking about? That's not how I remember it."

"Oh, it's not? Do you remember why we broke up?"

"Not really," I said.

"It's because Tammy Nigello offered to give you a blow job if you broke up with me."

"Oh yeah." She was right. I hadn't thought about that in years, perhaps since high school. "Holy shit, you remember that?"

"Of course I remember it! Don't friggin' laugh! I was pissed. I still am, kinda. Well, not really, I guess." She looked away. "So, did she?"

"What? Give me a blow job? I don't remember."

"Yes, you do. You asshole."

"It was pretty great, actually."

"Cocksucker."

"Yes, she was."

"You're such a dick!" she said and slugged me in the chest. She pulled out her phone and began reading a text.

"Husband?" I said.

"Yeah."

"Put it away," I said. "Tell me about your life. Two kids, right?"

She looked up and put her phone back in her purse.

"Yep, Janie and Henry. Henry's three. Cutest little boy you've ever seen."

"What's your husband like?"

"Lazy asshole, just like all of 'em."

"Oh Tina, tell me more about it."

"Fuck off," she said and laughed. "He's actually a great guy. He's great with the kids and he works hard."

"What does he do?"

"Do you really care?"

"Not really."

She laughed.

"I guess I want to know what your life is like together," I said.

"You want to know if we're happy."

"I guess so, yeah."

"We are. We're as happy as pigs in shit. What do you want me to say? I don't really think about it all that much. It's just life, Jimmy."

Cabs from the "Manzoni City Cab" taxi company started

lining up in front of The Bitter End.

Kenny Angelino walked over, exhaling cigarette smoke, smiling. Kenny was a former Metallica-crazed cigarette-smoking buzzard, now a raving Tea Party fanatic. I'd blocked him years ago on Facebook for posting pictures of Obama with a Hitler mustache and other ridiculous bullshit.

"Kenny!" Kelly said.

"It's Ken, now," he said. "How's the reunion going, Kelly? Didn't you guys used to date?"

"Once upon a time," she said.

"How's life, Ken?" I said.

"Life is good, Jimmy. How are you? Are you okay?"

What the fuck was that supposed to mean? Don't pretend to know what I'm dealing with, you simple-minded, uninformed asshole.

"How's life on the far right wing, Kenny? The world still ending under the Obama regime?"

"What?" he said.

"Obama's covering up a huge conspiracy to ruin America, right? We're all super duper fucked. The Socialist African nigger is going to kill us all. Isn't that what you assholes think?"

"What?" he said again. "Did you just call me an asshole?" He looked at me and took a drag on his cigarette. He looked like he wanted to throw a punch but thought better of it.

"He's just kidding," Kelly said.

"Whatever," he said. "He's all fucked up." He looked at Kelly. "You coming to The Hill? We're heading over now. We've got two kegs in the back of my truck."

"Awesome," I said. "We're in. See you there." He walked

away, smoking. He had those jeans with the threaded pattern and jewels knitted into the back pockets.

"Those are some bedazzled motherfucking jeans," I said. "Buzzard for life, I guess."

"What was that about?"

"What?" I said. "He's a fucking tool. He's racist too. You know that, right?"

"He was just trying to be nice. All he did was ask if you are okay. Are you?"

"I'm fucking fine. Totally fucking fine."

"Easy with the swearing. You don't really want to go to The Hill, do you?"

"Why not? Let's do it. Fuckin' walk down memory lane and all that. I'll grab Hogan."

"We don't have to," she said. It's "we" now?

"I want to go. Let's fucking go."

"Okay but you're not driving."

"No shit."

"I'll ride with you guys. Tina's too annoying right now."

We walked back into The Bitter End just as Rock turned off the music and jumped up on the bar.

"KEGGER AT THE HILL! I'M SHUTTING THIS PLACE DOWN IN FIFTEEN MINUTES! I'VE GOT FIFTEEN CABS LINED UP OUT FRONT! NO DRUNK DRIVING! SEE YOU BITCHES AT THE HILL!"

Kelly hopped in the backseat of Hogan's Impala and pre-emptively gave me shotgun. Hogan turned on the ignition.

"I'm fucking hammered," I said.

"Yep," Kelly said from the back.

"Ridiculous tolerance, huh, dude?" Hogan said.

"It just kind of hit me. I'm exhausted."

I leaned my head back against the headrest and closed my eyes.

When I woke I was alone in the front seat in the exact same position. I was still a little buzzed but also a little more sober and I felt better. I looked out the window, calculating my coordinates. I was at the end of the dead end on Elmwood Avenue at the base of the stairs to The Hill. The car was turned off. Nobody was around.

I got out of the car and could hear music and voices up The Hill. On my way up the stairs I saw a couple making out in the woods, midway up. When I got to the top there were dozens of people, mostly cliqued up in groups of five or six. Peter Dantonio was suddenly right in front of me offering me a hit from his joint.

"No thanks, man. I'm good."

"You just getting here?"

"Yeah. How long has it been since we left The Bitter End?"

"Fuck if I know," he said. "A few hours?"

"You having fun?"

"Fuck yeah! Blowing it out, bro! You need a beer?"

"Yeah, let's do it."

We walked over to a row of kegs entirely too large for a group this size and filled our cups. We turned around and faced the groups of former classmates.

"Dude," Peter said. "I think Tina's DTF."

"DTF?"

"Down to fuck."

"You guys dated for like two years, didn't you? You should do it. Just like old times."

"She's fuckin' psycho though, bro."

"All the more reason to do it. It's reunion weekend. It'll be electric."

"I know," he said and wandered off puffing his joint.

I stood there alone and surveyed the late-night crowd. I saw Hogan talking to the O'Brien twins and Z. No sign of Kelly.

I walked up to my former teammates.

"You fell asleep?" Sean said. "Old man!"

"How you feeling?" Hogan said.

"I'm good now," I said. "Even got a freshie." I held out my cup; Sean tapped it with his. I took one sip and it tasted warm and flat and disgusting and I tossed the beer out of the cup onto the grass.

"You guys really don't look that much alike," I said. "I used to think so but I don't anymore." Even though I'd spent an hour or two with them earlier playing lacrosse at the high school and eating pizza at Peppinos, it was as though I noticed this for the first time.

"The older we get, the less alike we look. I don't know why."

I looked up and saw Kelly, Tina, and Peter Dantonio talking. Kelly saw me and broke off and started coming our way.

"Oh my god," she said when she reached us. "I think Peter and Tina are gonna hook up."

"Nice!" said Sean.

"Is that a bad thing?" I said.

"She's such a mess right now. She's totally fucking up her life. They're both married but what do I care? She's a grown woman. She can do what she wants."

"That's right," I said.

"How are you feeling? Better?"

"Yeah. A lot."

"You were snoring like crazy," she said.

"Sorry about that."

"No, you must've been really tired. You nearly got into a fight with Kenny Angelino. Do you even remember that?"

"I remember."

"He almost ripped your head off."

"I know. He just set me off, somehow. He mentioned my kids and I just lost it."

I noticed everybody except Kelly looked down at the ground.

"No, he didn't," Kelly said. "He just asked if you were okay."

"Whatever. It doesn't matter now. I shouldn't have messed with him. He's probably a good person."

"He's a dick," Sean said. "But he's harmless."

"Still," I said. "Anyway, I just didn't realize how buzzed I was until I got into the car."

"We figured we'd leave you there all night," Hogan said. "And if the cops came you'd be the first one they'd arrest."

"Thanks, dick. Is it starting to get a little lighter out? What time is it?"

"Almost 5 am," Sean said. "I gotta hit the road. The kids will be up in an hour or two."

"Me too," his twin brother Michael said.

"Me too," Z said.

"I'll give you all a ride home," Hogan said. "Pile into the Imposter."

"Right on," Sean said.

We tossed our cups onto the ground, just like old times, and started walking toward the steps to Elmwood Avenue. On our way down, we heard the sounds of sex.

"Oh Jesus," Kelly said. "Gross."

"Somebody's getting some!" Sean yelled.

We kept descending and suddenly Peter Dantonio's ass came into view. Tina was facing the other direction, holding onto a tree while Peter jackhammered away.

All of the guys started laughing. Z whistled.

"Doggie style!" Sean said.

"Puppy love," Hogan said.

"Gross," Kelly said again, and we walked past them and down to Hogan's car.

Sean, Michael, and Z piled into the backseat and Kelly hopped on my lap in the front seat. I didn't know where to put my hands so I just kept them at my sides.

We drove off.

CHAPTER 8

In the weeks following college graduation, Jenny came to visit me in Syracuse for a weekend trip to Hogan's family cottage on the St. Lawrence River.

Jenny and I met in the fall of our senior year while we were both in other relationships, but by the end of that year during graduation week—a raucous week of morning, afternoon, and all-night parties mixed with carousing, vomiting, and ferocious and frequent hookups before the real world begins—we hooked up. It was mild and innocent and half drunken but we liked each other enough to exchange home addresses and phone numbers and we promised to get in touch. I would be moving to San Francisco later that summer and she would be moving to New York.

Jenny had written me a letter and suggested we get together that summer. The letter went on for several pages about how she didn't know what she wanted out of life but she figured that's how most people our age felt and hopefully New York would help her sort it all out. I remember being surprised at how forthright she was being about some of the larger questions in life given that we didn't know each other that well. The letter came on a Wednesday and by Friday afternoon she was in Syracuse and we drove the three hours north to the river on the Canadian border.

The Hogan family cottage was a tiny, two-bedroom wood cabin right on the river. Looking across the water you could see two of the "Thousand Islands" that dotted the river. That weekend we were joined by two of Hogan's brothers, their girlfriends, and Jessica, Hogan's girlfriend.

Not long ago I found a photo that was taken on that Friday afternoon. We were in the backyard of the house I grew up in and I was holding Jenny up. She was cradled in my arms and had her arms wrapped around my neck. Her hair hung down toward the ground and we were both smiling. I was wearing a seersucker button-down shirt, khaki shorts, and Birkenstocks—"hippie prep," Jenny later named it. She was dressed simply—a t-shirt, cutoff shorts, and flip-flops. Her legs were tan and beautiful, and as I looked at the photo I remembered how they felt in my arms that day and I remembered her smell too, and it was different from the scent I came to know in the many years of marriage that followed. There was a lush grape arbor in the background—a creation of my mother's that I hadn't thought about in years.

That evening we piled into Jenny's car, me driving, Jenny with an open beer in the passenger seat, and Hogan and Jessica in the back.

"So why did you and Lauren break up?" she said.

"I don't know," I said. "We got really serious and she wanted me to move in with her, but I figured we were too young for all that. I wasn't going to move in with her and get married and have kids, or whatever. I'm twenty-friggin'-two."

"I thought it was because she didn't have spice," she said and mimicked shaking a saltshaker onto a plate.

I laughed.

"You're right," I said. "No spice at all. Plus she was a planner. Jesus, always planning things, trying to get me to plan things. I'm not like that."

"Me neither."

"I guess not. You're here, aren't you?"

"That's right. Free to be you and me."

"Why did you break up with Brian?" I said.

"How did you know I broke up with him?"

"C'mon."

"Okay, I did. It was kind of the same thing. He wanted me to move to Florida with him while he started an entertainment company. He wants to represent bands."

"That sounds kind of cool, actually."

"I guess. But in the end I guess I didn't really love him enough to follow him."

"I guess that's pretty much the same with Lauren. I suppose if that part of it was there I would've moved in with her."

"No spice," she said.

"No spice."

We stopped at a grocery store on our way there and loaded up on supplies: watermelon, frozen pizzas, burgers, buns, and five cases of beer. When we arrived it was dark and the Hogan brothers went to work turning on lights, unlocking doors, and opening windows. Jenny and I put the groceries away and walked onto the deck with two freshly opened beers.

"The stars are insane out here," I said.

"Let's walk down to the water."

We left the Hogan brothers and their girlfriends behind and meandered down the dirt path to the dock on the water. The moonlight and stars made the water almost bright. We took our shoes off and sat on the end of the dock and hung our legs off the edge.

"What are you going to do in San Francisco?" she said.

"No idea. Dave Trammel's sister lives out there so we're going to crash with her until we find jobs. That's pretty much the extent of our plan." Dave Trammel was a lacrosse buddy from college.

"It's a plan, at least."

"Why, what are you going to do in New York?"

"No clue. My uncle lives in Tarrytown so I guess I'll stay with him until I figure out what I'm going to do. I want to work in an art gallery."

"That'd be cool."

"I guess," she said. "I kind of want to know what I'm going to do there. I don't need to have everything figured out but right now I've got nothing at all. I have no clue what I'm going to do there. Or with my life."

"Is it really that important to know what we're going to do with our lives? I mean, shouldn't we enjoy the not-knowing part?"

"It sounds like you've got it all figured out."

"Not at all. I have a degree in English and no clue what I'm going to do, but maybe we should embrace that."

"I guess. I'm still kinda scared, though. Or not really scared but just curious how it's all going to turn out. Aren't you?"

"For sure. But I also think one day we're going to die and on that day we'll know everything. All of the uncertainty of the future will be over and we'll have all of the answers to all of the questions we have now. We'll know how it all played out. Then it'll be all over. I say we enjoy the not-knowing. Just fucking thrust ourselves into the future and see what happens."

She leaned over and kissed me, then lay back on the dock and looked up at the stars.

"Let's sit here until we've seen three shooting stars," she said.

"Sounds like a plan," I said.

"Ha ha ha," she said. "Very funny. There's one."

"Do you ever think about living abroad?" I said.

"All the time. I want to travel everywhere. Greece, Turkey, Morocco, you name it."

"That's my plan, too. I kind of see San Francisco that way. It's so far from here it's almost like a foreign city. So I'll do that for a while and then just kind of go wherever life takes me. Morocco sounds good to me."

"I just want a life of adventure," she said. "That's why I couldn't move to Florida with Brian. Everything seemed preordained. I want to see the world."

"Then see the world you will," I said. "We're seeing it right now, in fact."

"That's true. There's another," she said, and another shooting star flashed and disappeared.

After a while we went back to the house and Hogan and his brother were playing guitar. I picked one up and we launched into "Willin'."

"You play?" she said.

I nodded and we all sang. Jenny didn't know the words but smiled throughout. When it was over she said, "That's a great song. I've never heard it before."

"'Stick with me, kid. I'll show you a good time.' That's what my mother always says."

She laughed and went to the fridge for more beers.

The next day when we were walking back to the cottage from the lake, I complimented the shape of her calves. They were perfectly drawn and tan.

"What?" she said. "Well, thanks. I guess you look at me the way I look at you."

"I guess so," I said.

CHAPTER 9

Elmwood Avenue was only two blocks from Kelly's parents' house, but she didn't ask to be dropped off first. I guess Hogan read the cue and asked the guys in back where they all lived. I had assumed these guys were still in touch—that everybody in Syracuse was still in touch with each other—but it wasn't like that. Hogan lived in Manlius. He hadn't seen these guys in years and certainly wouldn't know where they lived.

We dropped off Z and the O'Brien twins at their respective houses, and Kelly stayed seated on my lap even as the spaces opened up in the backseat. After the third drop-off I wondered if she would ask to be dropped off next. She didn't.

"Where to?" said Hogan.

"Let's watch the sunrise," I said.

"Cool. Where?"

"The Tennis Club," I said. "Let's go to the Tennis Club."

Sedgwick Farm Tennis Club was located on the street I grew up on. Yes, it was a private tennis club but I don't remember it as being elitist in any way—it seemed like everybody in the neighborhood was a member, and although

I don't know how much it cost to be a member, my middle-class parents were able to afford it. I took tennis lessons there when I was a kid and it was my place of summer employment all through high school. It consisted of nine red clay courts and members were required to wear white at all times.

"But we're not wearing white," Hogan said, smiling.

"Let's go sit on center court like we used to in high school."

In high school we would sneak into the club—I had the keys—and smoke pot on center court, a standalone court in the middle of the club that was used for all of the most important matches. One night in the summer before twelfth grade, Hogan and I went out there tripping on acid and performed an imaginary Wimbledon tournament without racquets or balls, playing out each point for an entire set while talking about the possibility (then likelihood, then certainty) of intelligent life in outer space.

"But first I want to see the house I grew up in. Ever since my parents moved I've never been back to see it."

"When was that?" Kelly said.

"Fifteen years ago."

We drove back to the old neighborhood and I remembered every detail. Driving down the street I grew up on I thought of the names of the families that lived in each house, some of whom were probably still there. We passed the Sedgwick Farm Tennis Club and pulled up in front of my old house.

"Wow," Kelly said. "It's been forever. I haven't been here since 9th grade. It still looks exactly the same."

And it did. The wood shingles were still painted brown;

the front door was still painted red; the garden my father had built in the side yard was still there.

We got out and walked through the side yard into the backyard. My mother's old grape arbor was still there, though it wasn't as lush as it was in that picture I'd recently seen of me and Jenny standing in front of it, maybe because of winter, maybe something else. It was dead quiet.

"I wonder who lives here," I said. "I wonder if they have kids."

Neither Hogan nor Kelly spoke. A few moments passed.

"Let's get out of here," I said. "I don't know what I was expecting to see."

We walked out to the front and up the street to the Tennis Club. When we arrived it was still mostly dark; it was just starting to get light. We hopped the fence one by one and walked out to center court. The red clay was dry and the courts were perfectly swept. The white lines were brushed and apparently recently painted, likely in preparation for the upcoming summer season—a duty I used to perform each spring. We sat in a line right in front of the net, Hogan and Kelly on either side of me.

"This has been the worst year of my life," I said. "I don't know how to move on."

"Do you have anybody to talk to about it?" Kelly said. I'd been wondering if Kelly knew about the accident because she'd said nothing about it. It occurred to me in that moment that she'd been acutely aware of it the entire night and had been watching out for me. This was probably why she was still with us sitting on center court at sunrise.

"No, I don't. But the problem is I don't want to talk about

it. I had a bunch of therapists and it was all a waste of time. I don't want to talk to anybody. I just want the feeling to go away."

"It won't if you don't talk about it," she said. "That's the whole point of therapy. You'll never not feel horrible about it but you'll learn to live with it."

"It's true, dude," Hogan said. "You've got to talk to somebody."

Of course, they were right. And so, without warning, right then and there, sitting on the red clay at center court as the sun started to rise, I started talking about it.

"It happened last spring. Just over a year ago. Jenny was up in Napa with some of her friends and I was watching the boys. We were heading to the grocery store to get a few things and we were sideswiped by a red SUV. Just like that. The motherfucker ran through a stop sign and bashed the shit out of us. The boys were killed instantly. I got banged up but the airbag saved me. It was the stupidest thing in the world."

"Jesus Christ," Kelly said. "That's horrible."

"Oh my God," Hogan said. "I never knew how it actually happened. Just that there was an accident."

"I mean, car accidents aren't all that dramatic. They happen every day. Somebody runs through a stop sign and your life is changed forever. Plus they weren't strapped in."

"Oh no," Kelly said. She started crying.

"Sometimes when we were just going really short distances I'd let them ride shotgun or play in the backseat. The grocery store was four blocks from our house in a residential neighborhood. I mean, 99% of the time I strapped them into their car seats. But all it takes is one asshole to run through a stop sign during the 1% of the time they weren't strapped in and that's that. I sued the shit out of the guy."

I was surprised by my own ability to talk about it. I'd hated talking about it in therapy in those early months in New York because it all seemed so pointless. What was done couldn't be undone by talking about it. But after telling the basic facts to Kelly and Hogan, I realized it actually did make me feel better to get it out there.

Kelly sobbed, though I was not crying myself as I spoke. In fact, I actually had an overwhelming sense that I should console Kelly, but instead I just sat there with my arms wrapped around my knees.

"It crushed my marriage. Jenny blames me for it and she's probably right. They weren't fucking strapped in. The grief was too overwhelming for her. She couldn't look at me from the moment it happened. She came back from Napa that night and never even hugged me. She just went ice-cold, and after the funeral she stopped talking to me altogether. I called for a little while after I moved to New York but by then she'd pretty much cut me off for good. We haven't spoken in months."

"I can only imagine how hurt she feels," Kelly said. "Losing your children. Jesus."

"Well, I'm here for you, dude," Hogan said.

"I know. Thanks, buddy. There's not much anybody can do, really. I just need to find a way to move on. I guess Jenny feels the only way she can move on is to cut me out. I can't blame her."

Kelly reached over and pulled me into her arms. She put

her face, wet with tears, up against mine and squeezed hard.

"You poor thing," she said. "You poor, poor thing."

It felt good. The red clay courts were clearly visible now as the night was replaced by that blue-grey early dawn light.

"Thanks," I said. "I'll get through it. At some point, I guess."

Kelly released my head, looked at me in the eyes from just a few inches away, and then hugged me again.

"It's okay," I said. "You don't have to."

"No," she said. "It's not even close to okay. You've been through the worst kind of tragedy and you can bet your ass I'm going to be here for you."

"You are here for me, Kelly. And I appreciate it, especially since I haven't seen you in like twenty years. Talking about it actually does make me feel better but I think I'm done now. I can only think about it in small doses."

Kelly released me and again looked me in the eyes from a few inches away. She nodded. "No problem. We're done then." She wiped her eyes.

The sun was coming up now and daylight allowed all of the surrounding houses, trees, and tennis courts to come into view. The night was going, going, gone.

"Hey," I said. "There's no way I'm going to be able to sleep anytime soon. Do you guys have anything to do tomorrow—today, I guess—or should we hit the Little Gem?"

"I'm not on duty again until Sunday night," Hogan said. "I'm in."

"All I've got to do is to listen to Tina's bullshit all day, then the reunion tonight. Oh my God. I just remembered that she screwed Peter Dantonio in the woods. Eck. Let's go."

We laughed and stood up and wiped the red clay off of our pants. Just then the sprinklers on the tennis courts popped up out of the clay and started watering the courts. We ran off and headed toward the exit.

"The 6 am watering. Still right on schedule," I said. "I swear, nothing in this town has changed."

"Except us," Kelly said.

"Except us," I said.

We hopped the fence again and piled into Hogan's Impala and headed to the Little Gem Diner—a Syracuse dining institution, at least for us. When we arrived Kelly sat next to me on my side of the booth. The Little Gem has that classic diner smell of coffee and hash browns and pancakes and omelets. It was a little run down—exactly as I'd remembered it. It was not any more or less run down than the last time I'd been there so many years ago.

Hogan looked at me and smiled. I don't know why.

"How the fuck did we fall out of touch for so many years, Hogan?"

"I don't know, dude," he said. "Life took over, I guess. Plus you never come back to visit."

"I know. I was so ready to get the fuck out of here after high school."

"Why is that?" Kelly said.

"I don't know," I said. "I was talking about this earlier with Z and the O'Brien twins. I guess I just wanted to see the world."

"That's bullshit," Hogan said. "Well, you probably did but that's not the whole story."

"I don't think so either," Kelly said.

"What?" I said.

"You were looking for something better," Hogan said. "You were trying to trade up."

"Well, yeah," I said. "That's probably true but what's wrong with that?"

"The more you look, the less you see," Hogan said. "Happiness comes from within. I got more where that came from if you want me to keep going."

"Yeah," Kelly said. "Earlier you were talking about 'these people' at The Bitter End. Like you weren't one of us. Look around. Just normal people eating breakfast. Are people at diners in San Francisco any different?"

I looked around. A construction worker. A man in a security uniform, likely just finishing his shift. A mother and daughter eating pancakes.

"Look, I'm not the pretentious dick you two seem to think I am. I just wanted to try out different things. I wanted to see the world. But it's funny now. I live in one of the most cosmopolitan cities in the world but most of the time I'm totally alone. Like, I feel totally alone."

"Maybe you should move back to Syracuse," Hogan said, laughing.

"Don't laugh," I said. "It might be good for me. But I don't see myself ever doing it. I think Syracuse served its purpose for me. It needs to live where it lives: in my past."

"Whatever works," Hogan said. "But yeah, we lost touch pretty much right after you left for college."

"No, I saw you every Thanksgiving and Christmas."

"That was really just a few times. You never came back

in the summers."

"That's true," I said. "I went to Martha's Vineyard every summer and waited tables with friends from college."

"Yeah, and once you moved to SF that was pretty much it."

"I guess that's true too," I said. "I guess I put Syracuse in my past and just kinda moved on. I'm not sure if it was intentional."

"I think it was," Kelly said. "You weren't one of 'these people,' at least in your mind."

"Maybe you're right. I don't know. And yet, it wasn't until tonight that I actually felt anything like myself since the accident. I owe you guys. At a minimum I'm buying this breakfast."

"See?" Kelly said. "We're not so bad."

"Well, I'll say this," I said and looked at Hogan. "There's no way I'm letting years go by again without staying in touch with you."

"Good," Hogan said. "Me neither."

After breakfast, I picked up the tab and we drove through the Syracuse morning toward home. I was in the front; Kelly was in the back. Freshly showered and shaved commuters were headed off to work as lights from stores started flickering on and coffee-shop doors swung open and closed. It was a short drive back to Kelly Donnatelli's parents' house where Hogan pulled up.

"Get out, Jimmy," she said. I didn't know what she meant. Get out of the car? Was I spending the night here? I got out of the car and turned toward her. She hugged me.

"You know I'm here for you, right?" she said.

"I know," I said. In that moment I wanted nothing more than to take her up to her childhood bedroom and have the best sex of our lives. We would re-create that afternoon in 9th grade in her twin bed. But this time we would do it with style, with passion, and none of the nerves of that forever-ago afternoon. Then I would fall asleep next to her and sleep for days. An erection tingled to life, as if of its own accord.

But that's not what she meant.

"You have a huge heart, Kelly Donnatelli. I really love you for that." What the fuck am I talking about? I thought. I haven't seen her in twenty years. And she's married. Stop being so clumsy. "I mean, I really appreciate you being there for me tonight and I really do feel better." Really this, really that. Stop rambling. "Get some sleep and let's hang together at the reunion tomorrow. Or tonight, I guess."

"Sounds good, Jimmy," she said and smiled.

I kissed her on the cheek and gave her another hug, holding back my hips.

"I'll see you tomorrow," I said.

"Get some sleep," she said.

I stood there and watched as she trotted up her old front porch. She stopped at her screen door and looked back at me. She smiled and flashed the peace sign again and went inside.

I plopped back in the car and shut the door.

"Take me home, dude," I said.

And Hogan did.

Part II

Saturday

CHAPTER 10

There's nothing in the world that can prepare you for witnessing the death of your own children. On top of that, in my case anyway, you could argue that I caused it and I can tell you with no-bullshit, mathematical motherfucking certainty that there's nothing in the world that can prepare you for causing the death of your own children. One moment you're driving to the grocery store at dusk and the next moment you're pulling the bodies of your two dead children out of your car.

I'm halfway through this damn thing so I guess I can't put off talking about it for much longer. Here's what happened.

We piled into the car and I announced that we didn't have to get into our car seats tonight. Charlie and Teddy cheered. We started driving and Teddy, my two-year-old, was sitting in the passenger seat and Charlie, my four-year-old, was standing on the backseat. Teddy's little legs hung over the edge of the passenger seat but didn't reach the floor. He was sucking his thumb—something that drove me crazy and that I'd told him a million times to stop doing—and holding on to his blankie. Charlie was standing in the middle of the backseat, between the two unused car seats, pretending like he was surfing and occasionally intentionally flopping himself down onto his car seat as if he'd fallen in the water, narrating and cheering. In the final moment before the red SUV blew through the stop sign and changed my life, I was watching Charlie through the rearview mirror while he said, "Look at me, Dad, I'm floating!"

Then, the crash.

The SUV was driving well over the speed limit—the son of a bitch was going 60 in a 30—and the police later ascertained that at the moment of the accident he was texting with his wife. I won't dignify the son of a bitch by printing his name here. It doesn't matter anyway. He smashed into my car on the passenger side, right where little Teddy was sitting. He hit our car with such force, the passenger-side door smashed into Teddy and pinned him between the door and the middle console. He was killed instantly. Charlie's head flew through the window in the backseat and broke his neck. He, too, was killed instantly. My airbag went off but I still bashed my head into my driver's-side window and slammed my left shoulder against the door as the airbag released. Needless to say, I survived. I didn't even break a limb.

I knew it was bad instantly but I didn't allow myself to think they were dead. I sprang into action as soon as the car stopped and I opened my door and pulled Teddy out with me. I laid him down on the grass, not willing to process the possibilities. I just laid him down and went straight back to the car and pulled Charlie from the backseat. I laid him down next to Teddy.

Having your children killed in front of you is so fucking

outside the realm of possibility, so far outside of anything you've ever experienced in your life that you don't accept it right away. I can remember moments passing where I was unconsciously considering alternatives. Of course they would've passed out from such a blow. Of course they'll wake up any second. It even seemed like they were still moving, however slightly.

I put my head to their chests, first Charlie, then Teddy, listening for a heartbeat. Nothing. I put my hand against their noses, feeling for breathing. Nothing. I felt their wrists and necks for a pulse. Then I gently shook Charlie, my older one, and his expression didn't change. A moment later I looked over at little Teddy and I knew it was over. I picked both of their limp bodies into my arms and sat with them, in shock.

"I've called 911," a voice said. I looked up and a woman on the sidewalk near me was holding her phone out at me as if to prove it. "They're on their way."

"Oh my God!" said another voice. It was the driver of the red SUV running toward me. "Are you okay?"

"They're dead," I said. "You killed them."

I don't remember feeling rage at that particular moment. I've since wondered why I didn't run at the guy and start beating the shit out of him. I should have. But instead I was so overwhelmed and shocked by what was happening I couldn't concentrate on anything at all. He was talking but I wasn't listening. The boys were still in my arms. I sat holding the dead bodies of my beautiful baby boys in a daze. I didn't even cry until the paramedics came and we rode together in the ambulance to the hospital. It was only then that I could allow myself to accept what had happened and let in the overwhelming sadness I would come to live with every day, up to and including today.

Just before then, the police arrived and the driver of the red SUV gave over his insurance information. The police officer told me he'd come speak with me at the hospital and to stay with the children. I didn't say anything to anybody until the children were checked in—already pronounced dead at the scene but checked in anyway to be confirmed by a doctor. Once they were, I called Jenny and told her to come home now. I didn't tell her exactly what had happened, only that there'd been an accident. She demanded to know if the boys were alright but I didn't tell her they were dead. I just told her to get home immediately.

The waiting was excruciating. Having full knowledge of what had happened felt more burdensome without having Jenny to share it with. I also dreaded telling her what really happened. Yes, it was an accident but they might not have died if they were strapped in. That's something we'll never know. I sat in the hospital waiting room crying on and off for two hours until Jenny arrived.

When she did and I told her everything, she went into a rage. I don't feel like reliving the exact conversation here. The bottom line is that from that moment forward she blamed me. She never spoke to me the same way again, and eventually she simply stopped speaking to me altogether. We all have our own way of dealing with tragedy, I guess.

In the months that followed I put a fair amount of time and energy into suing and, I'd hoped, prosecuting the driver of the red SUV. I wanted the son of a bitch to spend the rest of his life rotting in a jail cell. Unfortunately, texting while driving was not yet illegal in California, though I was able to press charges for reckless driving and gross vehicular manslaughter. I won't go into the legal details—a fucking shit show all around—but a jury ended up finding him not guilty of gross vehicular manslaughter and instead convicted him of the lesser charge of manslaughter with ordinary negligence. He originally faced up to six years in prison but now he'll serve less than one. He's serving right now, in fact. I didn't feel bad for his wife—she was the one he was texting with—and I wished he'd had kids so he could truly understand the torment he put Jenny and me through. But he never will. In the end, nobody won.

I didn't attend the trial because I couldn't bear to hear him talk about how bad he felt for killing my kids. Obviously that's what he would say. He'd put on a sad face and try and weasel out of it because the evidence was so overwhelmingly stacked against him. He'd even lied about the texting, but the police officer at the scene inspected his phone and found a half-written text on the floor of his truck. The stupid son of a bitch didn't have the sense to delete the evidence before the police came. He never even picked up his phone from the floor. He chose to spend that time telling me a bunch of apologetic bullshit I didn't listen to because I was in a state of shock. The stupid motherfucker was busted.

But in the end the jury fell for the apologetic bullshit and decided to reduce the charge and thus the sentence. The best decision I've made since the accident was not attending that trial. It went on for 14 days, and when my lawyer called me immediately after I learned that it played out exactly as I'd feared. When I read about it in the *Marin IJ* the next day

I had to endure descriptions of his crying wife and other family members standing around in a circle praying as the sentence was read. Fuck those people. Fuck all of them. I've heard of people who forgive those that do them the greatest harm. The woman who forgives her rapist. That father in Newtown who forgave that crazy fuck who shot his little boy. The families of the prayer group that white supremacist infiltrated and shot to hell. That's what Jesus would do. That's what truly religious people do. I'm not one of those people.

There was also an insurance settlement pending. My lawyer was dealing with that too and we'd been waiting to hear back when I was in Syracuse for the reunion. At that point, I didn't really have any expectation that it would play out any differently than the trial did. Busying myself with these punitive matters was nothing more than that: keeping myself busy. I suppose it was a way of distracting myself from accepting the hopelessness of it all. I suppose I thought that if I could win some small victory in court or from an insurance claim then I'd feel less worse. I never thought this consciously, but once the verdict came in I realized that's what I'd been doing. Without question, the whole process made me feel worse. C'est la vie, I guess. Even as I write this—again with some expectation that the writing will make me feel better—I know there's simply nothing to be learned from it.

CHAPTER 11

I woke up in my parents' guest bedroom. I could hear the TV on downstairs in my parents' little 2-bedroom, 2-level suburban condominium. I looked at the clock on the bedside table and it was 4 pm. Eight hours straight, I thought. I haven't slept for eight hours straight in over a year.

I turned on my phone and there were multiple voicemails from my lawyer (Bill) and a text from Jenny. A text from Jenny? It simply said, *Bill can't reach you. Call me.* I called Jenny immediately.

"Hello?" she said.

"It's me. What's going on?"

"Where have you been? We've been trying to reach you all day."

"Sorry, I slept really well for the first time in a year. My phone was off."

"Well, the insurance company called about the settlement," she said.

"What's the verdict?"

"Two million dollars ..."

"Holy shit."

"… per kid," she said.

"Holy fuckin' shit. Wow. I don't know what to say."

"I know."

"Oh, wow. I was … I was really just … I was really just trying to punish the driver," I said. I was stammering, talking in chunky fragments. "But Bill. Bill went after the money. It's good, I guess. I just don't know what to do with it. I guess you never have to work again. I actually don't even know if that's true. Or we could just give it away. I don't know."

"I don't know either."

"It's really good to hear your voice, Jenny."

She didn't say anything.

"How are you feeling about it?" I said.

"I don't know," she said. "I don't know how to feel about it. It's really strange." She paused, as if to choose the right words or to decide if she should tell me something. "I'm still really pissed at you but in a weird way I'm happy you did all of that work to get this money and put that asshole in jail. I didn't realize it until today, when I heard about the settlement."

"That's good. You know, I don't expect you to ever take me back, but ..."

She cut in. "I'm not going to."

"I know," I said. "I just want you to stop hating me."

"I don't hate you, Jimmy."

I paused. "Have you been seeing a therapist?"

"Of course," she said. "Haven't you?"

"No," I said. "I'm a fucking mess. But I want to see you. I want to talk about this in person."

"I think I do too, actually."

What did this make me feel? Shocked. Delighted. Scared. Instantly nervous.

"When? I can get on a flight tonight or tomorrow morning. I don't know if they have any flights here that leave tonight."

"Where are you?"

"I'm in Syracuse. My twentieth high school reunion is tonight."

"Oh Jeez," she said, and chuckled. She just chuckled, I thought. "Well, go to that and come out tomorrow. I don't hate you anymore, but I can't be with you ever again. We'll figure out what to do with the money and go our separate ways again."

"Okay," I said.

"Okay. Bye."

She hung up.

I went downstairs and my mother hopped up from the couch and hustled to the kitchen.

"Do you want some coffee, honey?" she said. "I've got it all ready to go."

"Yes, thanks, Mom."

"I'm so glad you slept! You know you left my car at Hogan's house last night but he came by and picked me up. So I've got it now. Nothing to worry about."

I hadn't even thought of it. I certainly wasn't worried.

"Who were you talking to just now?" she said.

I didn't want to tell her. I didn't want to have a big discussion about getting back together with Jenny and how badly we need each other and all that. But I told her anyway.

"Jenny."

"Oh, good!"

"She still doesn't want me back, Mom. But I am going out to see her tomorrow."

I didn't tell her about the insurance settlement. Withholding information from parents is an art form for children the world over.

"I bet she takes you back. You're the only person in the world who knows what she's going through. You're the only person who can truly help her."

I didn't respond. There was no point. I've known since I was a small child that there was no arguing with her. She thought what she thought and has never, ever been persuaded to change her mind based on facts and arguments. She was, and always will be, my mom.

She cooked me an omelet and we went back into the living room and watched MSNBC with my dad. Somebody somewhere was pissed about something somebody somewhere else said. Something about terrorists. Or maybe taxes. I couldn't concentrate, suddenly upended with this information about the four million dollars. I had no idea what we were going to do with it. This is a life-changing windfall. It could either change us for the better or change us for the worse, but only if we fought about what to do with it. I was thinking of it more as a way to reconnect with Jenny. Maybe this was my path back to her despite what she just said.

I listened to the half-dozen voicemails from my lawyer, all of which said essentially the same thing. The insurance company ruled in our favor. The money would be in my checking account next week.

"Holy fuck," I said.

"I know," my dad said, referring to MSNBC. I couldn't think straight.

I walked over to my parents' bar and poured a whiskey, neat.

CHAPTER 12

The first year we were married was the most productive year of my life. We were living in Sausalito in a tiny duplex with a beautiful view—a "view with a room," Jenny used to say. It had wind and saltwater-beaten brown weathered shingles and the entire front of the house was all windows. You could see Angel Island from our living room and bedroom, which were both at the front of the house, connected by a wooden deck. At night the moon reflected on the water and boats floated by in silhouette.

Sausalito was a place I'd taken to many years before. When I'd get burned out on the city—work, people, parking—I'd drive over to Sausalito and walk along the water and explore the local scene, alone. On one such day I was totally fed up with my middle-management position at a struggling Internet company and woke with the feeling that I needed to quit. It was right in the middle of the dot-com bust and jobs were scarce, but I was totally burned out. I called in sick and decided to drive to Sausalito for breakfast. I ended up sitting one table away from Bob Weir of the Grateful Dead, one of my all-time favorite musical heroes, who was eating with

Woody Harrelson. For thirty-five minutes I debated talking to them while I ate my breakfast and read my book. I wanted to be cool about it, to leave them alone to enjoy their breakfast in peace and almost did. But when they got up to leave I simply said, "I don't want to hold you up but I'm a big fan. I've been to dozens of shows. The way you kept going after Jerry died was inspirational to me. I sound like an idiot. Have a great day."

He smiled and simply said, "Thanks. The main thing is to keep going." And off he went.

I didn't quit that job, and in the year that followed I took advantage of the small opportunities at that shitty Internet company and ended up setting myself up well for a much better opportunity at a new company. I like to think it was because of Bob Weir.

On another occasion while Jenny and I were living together in Russian Hill, I walked from our apartment through the Marina and over the Golden Gate Bridge to Sausalito contemplating whether I should ask her to marry me. It was a beautiful summer day with just the right amount of breeze, and by the time I got to Sausalito I decided Jenny was the best person in the world for me and I'd be crazy not to do it. It was on that day that I decided we needed to move across the Bay to this beautiful little seaside town.

We moved there two months after the wedding and thus began an unexpected creativity surge. I began writing. I buddied up with a reader/writer friend from work and over the course of that year we each wrote a novel. Mine wasn't very good (his was better), but it was a really fun and rewarding experience to actually get something down. Maybe someday

I'll revisit it and try and get it published.

I also started writing a lot of music. Our friends were all in the city but quickly adapted to driving out to Sausalito to hang out with us and play music. We had weekend day parties on a regular basis—we grilled, drank beers, and had acoustic guitar jams all day long and into the night. Most of my best friends all played and Sausalito seemed to usher in a creative period for all of us. We began writing song after song after song, individually, and unveiling them at these afternoon Sausalito jam sessions. Weekend after weekend we surprised each other with new songs; some were actually good. Then we'd all learn each other's songs and create guitar solos and bridges and lyrical improvements and background vocals, and we'd iterate on this bulging catalogue while the girlfriends and wives and friends popped in and out of the musical living room.

On one such Saturday not long after the wedding, I started the day by making breakfast for Jenny and bringing it to her in bed. It seemed like a romantic thing to do. I didn't have a tray so I brought in the plate with the omelet and fruit on the side and set it on her lap while she sat up in bed, then I left to fetch the coffee and orange juice and set the two mugs on the crowded bedside table. She took a bite and some of the fruit spilled off the plate and onto the duvet. When she tried to take a sip of orange juice she had to balance the plate on her lap while reaching for the juice, trying not to twist her torso too much. She started laughing.

"It doesn't really work, does it?" I said.

"No, it's great!"

I reached to pick up the plate from her lap. "Let's eat on

the deck. It's a beautiful morning."

"It was a sweet gesture. It just sorta sucked in practice."

We both laughed.

As I was removing the plate from her lap she grabbed it from me and tossed it on the bedroom carpet, spilling everything. She laughed and I laughed, half-shocked at the omelet on the carpet, and she pulled me into the bed.

Our marriage was off to a good start.

CHAPTER 13

I was standing at my parents' bar sipping whiskey when Hogan called.

"You ready, my brother?" he said.

"What's the plan?"

"I'm taking you someplace special for dinner. Then off to good old Thomas Jefferson 'let's get' High."

"Good old Thomas Jefferson 'let's get' High. I haven't thought about that in years. Sounds good, man. I've got some seriously fucked-up news I want to talk about."

"On my way."

While I waited for Hogan, I sipped my whiskey behind the one-man bar in my parents' compact suburban condominium living room and pondered the multiverse of possibilities splayed out before me. Four million dollars. Unbelievable. But what I really wanted to know was what it would mean for Jenny and me. What would she want from it? What could I do to give her whatever it was she wanted from it? Unknowable, and yet, I felt like I needed to solve it. Nevertheless she'd made it clear we were done. I was torn between wanting to solve it and throwing in the towel and accepting the rejection she'd made perfectly clear.

"Is there anything else I can get you, honey?" my mother said.

"I'm good, Mom."

"So what's the plan for the big reunion?"

"I don't really know. Hogan's on his way over now to pick me up and take me to some mysterious dinner and then we're off to good old Thomas Jefferson High.

"Thomas Jefferson 'let's get' High?"

"You know about that?"

"Are you kidding? Mothers know everything."

Move on. "After that, there's some sort of after-party I have no interest in so I'll probably be home early. I've booked a 9 am flight for SFO tomorrow morning so I'm sort of focused on that.

"And understandably so. Jenny probably can't wait to see you."

"Mom, stop."

"You don't know how women think, honey. You think you do. But you don't."

I didn't reply. She was certainly right about that, though obviously wrong about Jenny.

"Anyway, sorry this trip was so quick. I thought I'd have all day tomorrow to lounge around with you guys but I obviously had to change my evening flight back to New York and head out to SF. It just couldn't be helped."

"I totally understand, honey. I'm so happy you're going out to see Jenny. It's absolutely the right thing to do."

It's funny thinking back on it now. In that moment my mother had no idea about the four-million-dollar settlement and didn't at all question why I was suddenly flying out to San Francisco early Sunday morning to see my estranged wife after an entire year of near-zero communication. That's how badly she must've wanted us to get back together. Funny to think about it now.

A few minutes later, Hogan knocked on my parents' door. My mom let him in and gave him a hug.

"Here he is!" she said. "The most eligible bachelor in Manlius."

"I wish," Hogan said, laughing.

"You're not gay, are you? It's okay to be gay. I love the gays. They're so good to their mothers."

Hogan looked at me, laughing. "You are your mother's son, that's for sure."

Hogan and I headed out.

"Check this out, dude," Hogan said as we drove off. He hit "play" on the car stereo. I immediately knew what it was.

"Eyes opener," Hogan said. "Remember this?"

"Oh my God," I said. "I'll never forget."

June 17, 1991. Giants Stadium. Hogan, Theo, Mikel, and my girlfriend at the time, Mary Ginello, went down in a van my father procured for us from a friend. A ragtag group of teenagers (well, that's how we saw ourselves) drove all the way from Syracuse to East Rutherford, New Jersey, to see two Dead shows. We got there early, found doses of acid, and partied all afternoon in the lot before experiencing what was later considered one of the best Grateful Dead shows of the final years of the band. Commenters on archive.org and YouTube have since said this was the last truly great show before it all ended in 1995.

"I remember it rained during the first set," Hogan said. "Remember those seats we scored? And then it cleared up and we headed up to our actual seats on the upper deck and rocked the second set. That's when you pulled out the hash nobody knew you had."

"I remember. It was totally random. We got split up on our way into the show. Remember? Me, Mary, and Mikel headed toward our seats but you and Theo tried to find a spot under the overhang to avoid the rain. On the way to our seats some hippie offered me hash and I bought it in about 30 seconds. Hash? Yes! $20? Done! And that was that. We were tripping our balls off and Mikel was determined to find you guys. Plus it was raining so Mary and I were on board. We fuckin' traversed that stadium and randomly saw you guys standing in a totally empty row under the overhang out of the rain. It was unbelievable. 70,000 people standing in the rain and you guys find an entire empty row under the overhang. Ridiculous. And we found you! Right as the 'Eyes' opener started. The timing couldn't have been better if we'd planned it. The days before cell phones, man."

"I know," Hogan said. "Theo was just leading me deeper and deeper into the stadium with all of these hippies everywhere twirling and shit. I had no idea where we were going. Then all of a sudden he was like, 'Oasis!' and he led us to that empty row under the overhang. I can't believe you guys found us."

"I know," I said. "It was all Mikel. I miss him so much. That fucker had balls. A real sense of adventure."

Mikel died a few years after that. You'd think he'd die hang-gliding naked over the Ganges or something but it was more mundane than that. He contracted stomach cancer and was dead less than three months after his diagnosis. Just like that.

"He was the best," Hogan said. "One of a kind."

We drove on in silence. After a while I said, "Where are we going?"

"Surprise, dude."

"Okay."

"What was the crazy thing you wanted to tell me about?" Hogan said.

I told him about the settlement, about the guy in jail, and about going to see Jenny tomorrow.

"Wow, dude. Four million dollars! That's amazing. You must be psyched!"

"I'm stunned," I said. "I don't know what to do about it. That's what I'm hoping Jenny and I will figure out in the next few days. But to be honest, I don't even really know if I want Jenny back. I mean, I do, but she said we'd decide what to do about the money and then go our separate ways again. She made it 100% clear that she's never going to take me back. So what the fuck am I supposed to do? Wait around forever?"

"You're asking the wrong guy about relationships. And after everything you two have been through there's nobody who can tell you what you should do. Go with your gut, I guess."

"I guess," I said.

We drove on. Where to, I didn't know.

CHAPTER 14

In the fall of my high school freshman year, I attended
my first high school dance. Kelly Donnatelli and I were
dating and agreed to meet there. Hogan and I skateboarded
there and when we arrived I remember feeling nervous. Did
I have to dance? Would Kelly and I make out?

We'd kissed three times since we started dating two
months before. I'm not sure you'd call it making out. It was
more like conquering a fear than a romantic experience. The
very first time we kissed we just pressed our lips together for
about five seconds and concluded with one smooch. It was
nothing more than a prolonged smooch. The second time
we went for the tongue touch—your classic French kiss. It
was exhilarating and her tongue felt much smaller and softer
than mine must've. The third time was another French kiss,
but we simply held our tongues together for a few seconds
longer—a prolonged French kiss. At my first high school
dance in the fall semester of my freshman year, I wondered if
we'd finally make out.

There were dozens (hundreds?) of kids at the dance,
some milling around in the hallway but the vast majority

milling around inside the darkened gymnasium. Less than half of the students were actually dancing. Nobody really dances at dances, I figured. I should be okay. I remember the exact song that was on when we first arrived and it might've been "Cruel Summer" by Bananarama. Why I remember this random detail is a mystery. I looked around for Kelly until I spotted her standing against the wall with Tina, her ever-present best friend. Hogan teamed up with Mikel and Theo and hung out in the well-lit hallway while I entered the gym and approached Kelly and Tina. I got over to them at the exact same moment as Peter Dantonio, everybody's grade school best friend.

"Jimmy!" Peter said. "Let's ask these ladies to dance!"

I looked at Kelly, standing perfectly still, slightly panicked, trying to focus on her face in the dark gym. The song that was playing was way too fast for me to dance to. It was "It's Tricky" by Run DMC. I remember it clearly.

"Aren't you going to ask me to dance?" she said.

The song ended. Thank God. "Take It to the Limit" by the Eagles came on. Thank God more.

"Okay. Dance?" I said.

"You are too funny. You're so shy." She grabbed my hand and led me to the dance floor. We coupled up and started waddling from side to side, my hands around her waist, her hands around my neck. I immediately sported a woody that pressed into her belt buckle. I put my chin on her shoulder and she leaned in and kissed my neck. I have forever loved "Take It to the Limit" and forever will.

After the song ended, "Mony Mony" by Billy Idol came on. Peter and Tina stayed on the dance floor while Kelly grabbed my hand and led me off. Moments later I realized we were headed toward the huge stack of folded-up bleachers. When we got to the corner of the gym there was a space behind the bleachers just large enough for us to walk behind. We walked about ten feet in and, it's safe to say, we made out. Our mouths clashed together, wide open, and we thrashed our tongues back and forth, up and down, side to side, in and out with no rhythm whatsoever. It was a rapid-fire tongue assault, a medieval sword fight inside our gaping mouths. It was inelegant. It was sloppy. It was amazing.

It may have gone on for hours had our 9th-grade geometry teacher not tapped me on the shoulder and wordlessly motioned for us to get out of there. Much to our surprise we didn't get in trouble in any way. We were merely released back into the sweaty adolescent scrum of the freshman dance in the dark gymnasium.

In the months following that dance we made out as often as we could, usually after school at her house, and we nearly perfected the skill. Little by little we went a little further—a hand up the shirt and so on. But for me, that night behind the bleachers, recklessly making out to "Mony Mony" by Billy Idol, was the beginning of something.

CHAPTER 15

We pulled up to a convenience store I'd never been to before and Hogan parked the Impala.

"What's up?" I said. "Beer run?"

"Get out," Hogan said.

"Just let me give you some money for the beer. I like this tune," I said, pointing at the stereo. "Or are you the weak-ass kind of alcoholic who can't even handle buying beer without falling into a weeklong drunken stupor?"

"Fuck you, dick. Get out and shut up. Follow me."

Hogan got out of the car and was all the way to the convenience store door before I finally got out. We walked into the convenience store and a tattooed Goth girl with jet-black hair and a nose ring was ignoring us from behind the counter. She wasn't a day over 25.

"Can I help you?" she said without expression.

"Bodega," Hogan said.

"Oh, here we go," I said. "I'm not interested in the whole 'Eyes Wide Shut' thing. Thanks, though."

"IDs," she said. We handed them over. She barely looked at them, handed them back, and reached under the counter.

We heard a loud click and she walked a few steps to her left and opened an otherwise industrial and undecorated door.

"See, dude? A surprise."

We walked down two flights of stairs into a basement with soft orange lighting. There were antique-looking paintings and furry animal heads on the walls. I noticed a table with a record player on it, the record spinning. Talking Heads. *Stop Making Sense.* Side 1. I could smell the scents of both whiskey and, separately, cheese melted on toast.

"So hip," I said. "Speakeasies are all the rage these days, aren't they? Even in Syracuse."

The room was narrow with a bar on the left and tall booths on the right, separated by a narrow aisle where an unusually beautiful waitress stood over a table. Long brown hair, long legs, light brown skin, possibly Hawaiian, possibly Japanese, possibly a mix of both. Very short cutoff jean shorts. Hogan started walking directly toward her, and as we got closer I could see who she was talking to sitting in the high-backed booth.

"Holy shit," I said. "No fucking way!"

"Surprise!" Theo said.

Theo got up from the booth and gave me a hug. The beautiful waitress was looking at us, smiling.

"Theo! I thought you lived in Thailand or some shit!"

"I did," Theo said. "But now I'm back. For good, I think."

"When? Where were you last night?"

We separated from the hug but each kept one hand on the other's shoulder.

"*I've been all around this whole round world,*" he sang. "*And I just got back today.*"

"Ha. Amazing. It's so great to see you, dude," I said. "It's been forever. So you're back?"

"Have a seat. Niko will bring us some drinks." He looked up at her. "Two Laphroaigs and a Coke for Hogie boy."

"You got it, babe," the beautiful Niko said, flashing another wide smile before walking away. All three of us watched her like teenagers as she glided away. Hogan and I sat in the oversized booth across from Theo.

"It's so great to see you, dude," I said again.

"You too, Jimmy," Theo said.

"How did that happen? How did so many years go by?"

"I don't know, dude," Theo said. "Who knows? It's just life, I guess."

"I know," I said. "I just feel bad about it. I've got all of these distinct groups of friends—college friends from Vermont, San Francisco friends, you guys. It's weird how you can just fall out of touch like that."

"I know. We were all best friends for years and years but then life just keeps barreling on, you know? It's not like we had Facebook or whatever back then. We didn't even have the Internet when we stopped hanging out. We saw each other almost every day for the first 17 years of our lives and then not at all. You went to San Francisco. I went to Thailand. It happens."

"I guess so. You didn't even come to my wedding, man. You've never even met Jenny. But why doesn't it feel like that much time has passed? I still feel like we're all best friends."

"Same here," Hogan said. "We're just older."

"It is what it is, I guess," Theo said.

"It doesn't matter now," I said. "Here we are."

"Here we are!" Theo said.

"So what brings you back from the paradise jungles of Thailand to cold, shitty Siberacuse."

"I'm going to start a restaurant," Theo said. "Northern Thai food only. No bullshit. No pad thai and no fried spring rolls. No 'American Thai.' Real northern Thai food. It's the best food in the world and nobody's ever had it. After fifteen years of living back and forth between here and there, mostly there, I feel like my cooking skills are good enough for me to strike out on my own. No more working in other people's restaurants."

"That's great, dude. But why here? Why Syracuse? Why not New York or San Francisco? Too expensive?"

"Because this is my home. I could open up this place there and it'd be a huge hit. I'm telling you, this is a fucking lay-up. Expensive isn't really the problem. I just wanted to be home."

The distinctive chords of The Cars'"Let the Good Times Roll" came on the stereo. Hogan began tapping out the drum track on the table.

"Amazing," I said. "It's amazing how many dudes from our high school decided to stay or come back."

"Everything's just really familiar feeling. After all of those years in these little villages in Thailand or raging in Bangkok I need that feeling of home. You know?"

"I do, actually," I said. "But for me that feeling is in San Francisco. Sausalito, really. I mean, everything's super familiar here but in a different way. I think my soul is in San Francisco."

"So that's where you're living now?"

"No, New York."

"Oh, I just figured ..."

"I know, it doesn't make sense," I said. "I don't know what the fuck I'm doing in New York. I'm pretty miserable there actually. I'm heading out to San Francisco tomorrow and hopefully I'll never even go back to New York. In fact, I'm not going back to New York. I think I just decided that right now."

"Don't you have to work?" Theo said. Hogan smiled and sang along to The Cars. "*Let them brush your rock-n-roll hair, let the good times roll.*"

"We'll see," I said. "I just came into some money. Long story. I had kids, they died in a car accident, my wife left me, and I ended up with some money. That's basically it. I just found out today. About an hour ago, actually."

"Okay," Theo said. "Well that ain't nothing." Niko arrived and put our drinks on the table. She smelled delicious. She also placed three food menus on the table in a single stack.

"Crossroads time, dude," I said.

Theo raised his glass. "To crossroads," he said.

"Indeed," I said, and all three of us clanked our glasses and took big sips.

We ordered from the minimalist menu—melted Havarti cheese on artisan toast, deviled eggs with paprika and cayenne, miniature lamb meatballs and yogurt, Kobe sliders—and caught up on all manner of things from the last two decades. The bartender, too old to be a hipster but otherwise having all the qualities of one, kept a steady flow of '70s and '80s vinyl playing, rotating through the first side of record after record. *London Calling, The Rise and Fall of Ziggy Stardust and the Spiders from Mars* (still a favorite of mine), *Credence Clearwater Revival's Greatest Hits, Born to Run, Sticky Fingers, 1984, Breakfast in America.*

After eating for a while I said, "Every single record this guy has played was in my childhood record collection. Like, all before I discovered the Dead in 11th grade. These records are all so great. And in college I told my parents they could throw them all out when they sold the house, thinking records were dead. Now they're all the rage again."

"Along with speakeasies," Hogan said, smiling.

"Yeah, well," Theo said. "Northern Thai restaurants are next. Trust me."

"You're probably right," I said. "Maybe I'll be your first investor. My wife … ex-wife? separated wife? I don't know what she is … anyway, we need to figure out what we're going to do with that money first. That's why I'm going to San Francisco tomorrow."

"Not that you need it but you'll make a fortune on that investment," Theo said. Theo wasn't the type to bullshit, at least he wasn't back when we were teenagers, and I tended to believe him on this one. He was generally uncompromising, in fact. If he didn't want to do something, he didn't do it. He never settled. I remember he turned down a flat-out proposition for sex from Tammy Nigello because she wasn't up to his standards. No other guy I knew turned down sex in high school. It was all coming back to me.

"I believe you," I said. "What did you do in Thailand for all those years? Just cook?"

"Pretty much. The first year I lived off some savings I had

and just wandered around Bangkok."

"Banging cock?" I said.

"Shut up," he said. "That's an old one. And not even funny."

"I know," I said. "Continue."

"Well, after a while in Bangkok I learned the language and was able to get further and further away from there. Eventually I ended up in the north and started working in kitchens. Mostly mom-and-pop joints. I got stoned every day, ate like a king, and just chilled. It was great, man. Years went by."

"Did you have any girlfriends?" Hogan said. "Or was it just a little sucky sucky from the farmer's daughter kind of thing? Me love you long time."

"A little bit of both. I never paid for it, though. Fuck that. The women there are beautiful," he said. "The ones I dated, anyway."

"I'll bet," I said.

The opening chords of "Rocks Off" came on. *Exile on Main Street.* Side 1.

"The crew back together," Hogan said. "I can't believe it."

"How about a cheers for Mikel, the only missing link," I said.

"A round of shots," Theo said. "Niko!" he called. "Two grappas and a shot glass full of lemon juice for Hogie boy!"

"You got it, honey," Niko said.

"You're gonna hook up with that beautiful waitress, aren't you?" I said.

"Already did, buddy," Theo said. "Last night and again this morning. I'm hoping she's going to be my new girlfriend."

"I thought you just got back today?"

"That might have been a little white lie. But look at her. Priorities."

"You're going to be a huge fucking success," I said. "You know that?"

"Yep. I do. But just so we're clear about Niko. She chose me. She's obviously way out of my league. And it's probably more than just sex, despite me trying to sound cool."

Niko brought the shots and we cheersed to Mikel while The Rolling Stones sang about kissing (something or other) in Cannes.

"Tonight doesn't have to suck," I said. "Tonight could be epic if we want it to be."

"And why should we settle for anything less?" Theo said.

We drank the shots.

"So how is it possible that there's a smokin' waitress, probably in her early 30s, still single in Syracuse?" Hogan said. "I've been looking for that chick for years."

"She's got a kid," Theo said. "He's 10. Most guys don't want to deal with somebody else's kid."

"There's always a catch," Hogan said.

"But I don't think it bothers me," Theo said. "I've probably got a few kids running around out there that I don't know about. I'm kidding, obviously, but maybe I should be a father figure to him."

"But you're one of the least responsible people I know," I said. "Or you were, anyway."

"I'm turning over a new leaf, Jimmy. I'm about to turn 40 and it's time to get my shit together. It's not like there's anybody pushing me, either. I'm just ready. Niko and her little boy might be just the thing for me."

"Well," I said, "there's nothing like kids to make you get your ass in gear. I don't know what it's like to raise a 10-year-old but I bet you'll be good at it."

"I think so," Theo said.

"Plus you get to have sex with her," Hogan said, pointing at Niko as she walked by.

"On balance," Theo said, "it's a good deal. She's very cool."

"So what's the plan?" I said.

"I just told you," Theo said.

"No," I said. "I mean for tonight."

"It's 8:30," Theo said. "Holy shit, we've been here for like three hours. Well, I think we should do one more round here and then head up to Tommy J. for the thing."

"I totally forgot about the reunion," I said. "But yeah, let's go. It'll be funny to see everybody again. I seriously can't remember anybody's names."

"Me neither," Theo said. "Let's go in there and see what that's all about. If it sucks we'll just leave. We can come back here or we can get stoned and just drive around. I've got some great bud."

"Let's go with the flow," I said.

We left the hipster speakeasy beneath the convenience store and piled into Hogan's Impala—Theo in front, me in back. We drove toward our old high school. Theo lit up a joint and it smelled more like incense than pot. A deep, perfumed blend of spices with marijuana as its base.

"That smells amazing," I said.

"It does," Hogan said. "But I can't. Well. No. I really can't."

Theo held it up between the two front bucket seats without a word.

"I really shouldn't," I said.

"You really should. I can't think of anybody more in need of this than you right now."

I took the joint between my thumb and forefinger. Warm smoke drifted upward in a thin, bluish wispy stream, breaking into multiple directions as it collided with the Impala's closed glass sunroof. I inhaled. The smoke felt smoother on my throat than I'd remembered. I exhaled.

"One hit is all I need," I said and handed the joint back to Theo.

"Good call, especially if you never smoke. This is the real deal."

Within moments I started feeling better, lighter. It wasn't the fuzzy, faraway feeling from the stoned high school and college years, but something different. I felt clear.

"This pot is incredible," I said. "I can actually think straight. And I can talk."

"It's the best," Theo said. Hogan laughed, rolled down his window, and turned up the radio. Theo rolled down his window and we sang along with the Dead through the cool spring night. House after house, more and more of them recognizable from childhood, passed by while we sang. By the time we got to the high school parking lot I was feeling fully lucid with a happy glow underneath.

The parking lot was packed—no spots anywhere near the gym entrance. We drove out past the football/soccer/lacrosse field I'd played lacrosse on both last night and all those years ago and parked at the nearest spot. As we walked toward old Thomas Jefferson High I was surprised by how big the school seemed. It was fortress-like, with concrete covering the top half of the school and grey bricks covering the bottom. In the daylight the school is brown and grey, but as we approached from a distance it looked colorless, like a faded replica of itself.

We entered the school gymnasium through the propped-open double-wide doors, and we walked through turned-off metal detectors into the brightly lit hallway outside the gym. We walked past the high school girls working the welcoming booth, not bothering to get our nametags. There were smatterings of people chatting in the hallway, and inside the gymnasium the event was in full swing, the lights turned down low. "Bust a Move" was playing. I could see Kelly and Tina talking in there, off to the side.

"Let's hang out here for a bit," Theo said. "I've got to get my shit together before I go in there."

"I'm going in," I said.

"Ha. I see how it is," Hogan said and looked over at Theo. "I'll hang with you out here."

I walked into the gym toward Kelly and Tina.

"Jimmy!" Kelly said. "You look happy."

I didn't realize I'd been smiling as I approached. "Just stoned," I said.

"Awesome!" she said and laughed.

"Who's holding? Theo?" Tina said.

"Yeah, Theo. He's out there with Hogan," I said, gesturing toward the hallway. Without a word, Tina was off.

"Thanks for last night," I said. "It was great to reconnect with you. I really appreciate you staying out all night and listening to my stuff."

"Jimmy, please," she said. "It was my pleasure. You've been through a lot and even though we haven't seen each other in God knows how long, you're still really important to me. I've thought about you nonstop since I first heard about it."

"Thanks," I said. "It's weird. I came here to forget about it and instead last night actually helped me process it, just a tiny little bit. I guess it was talking to old friends, people I hadn't seen in ages. I really can't thank you enough."

I was surprised at how chatty I was. Pot never used to feel this way. It was almost the opposite of how I remembered it. Not only was the paranoia gone, I had a strange form of confidence.

"You know," I said, "I really wanted to kiss you good-bye last night, but I didn't want you to think I was taking advantage after you'd been so nice to me."

She laughed but didn't respond. I looked away.

"Should we dance?" she said.

"To this?" I said. Rob Base was playing. "It Takes Two."

"Why not?" she said. "C'mon, Jimmy, it'll be fun." She grabbed my hand and started swaying while walking backwards toward the middle of the gym, which passed for a dance floor as it did in high school. Before we got there, the song ended.

"Thank God," I said. "Please give me a slow song."

"You haven't changed a bit!" she said.

As if on cue, "In Your Eyes" by Peter Gabriel came on. We put our arms around each other and started slow dancing. I didn't recognize any of the dozen or so people dancing around us.

"Oh my God," she said. "Our song. Do you remember?"

"You mean the scene in *Say Anything*?" I said.

"No, dummy. This song. This was our song."

"What? We had a song? Were we living in a romantic comedy? We did not have a fucking song."

"Yes, we did!" she said. "And this was it! I guess it does sound ridiculous but whatever, we were in 9th grade. One time when we were making out in my bedroom we were playing this record—*So* by Peter Gabriel, remember?—and you said this song reminded you of me."

"Oh my God. So cheesy. I always did love your eyes but Jesus, what a terrible line."

"Well, I fell for it. It was then that I decided to go all the way with you, although it still took me four more months to work up the nerve to actually do it."

"I definitely remember that," I said.

"I'll bet you do. And let the record reflect this was our song BEFORE *Say Anything* came out and ruined it."

"Duly noted. I can't believe you remember all that, Kelly."

"I remember everything," she said.

"You know what I remember?" I said.

"What?"

"Making out behind those bleachers over there."

"Oh my God! The sloppiest kiss of all time!" she said.

"It was practically violent," I said. "We didn't know what we were doing. It's really the first kiss I remember. I'm pretty sure it was my first real make-out session."

"Mine too," she said. We continued to sway side by side as the chorus kicked in. *And all my instincts, they return.* This really was turning into a bad movie.

"Let's do it again," I said. "Right now."

"What?" she said.

"Right now. Let's go behind those bleachers and have a real kiss—the kind of kiss we would've had if we'd known what we were doing when we were fourteen. We owe it to our 9th-grade selves."

"Really?" she said.

"Apparently our song is playing."

She laughed and opened her eyes widely, surprised at the possibility of what was about to happen. In that moment I wasn't sure what she was thinking. She was married. She had kids. She certainly wouldn't have wanted to jeopardize all of that. On some level I too was married. I had had kids. But what was at stake, exactly? There were witnesses everywhere. Rather than open up a discussion weighing the pros and cons, she looked around, as if to see if there was a high school geometry teacher waiting in the wings to bust us. This time around there would be no cost/benefit analysis, and without a word she grabbed my hand and started walking toward the bleachers in the corner of the dark gym.

And while Peter Gabriel sang perhaps the most iconic, cheesy, overused high school romance song of the 1980s, we faced each other behind the bleachers and kissed. We were in no hurry, happy to be here and only here, enjoying a moment twenty-three years in the making. Eventually, our lips parted and we both started laughing.

"I can't believe we just did that."

We stood there with our arms around each other behind the bleachers while the music played.

"Holy shit," Kelly said, and broke away. "Fuck. I have a

husband. I have kids."

"Don't think about that. It's just a kiss. For old time's sake."

"No. I need to get out from under these bleachers. Fuck!"

She turned away from me and hustled out from under the bleachers back into the dark gymnasium. I followed her and noticed "Under Pressure" was playing and the dance floor was more filled up than when we'd been dancing to "In Your Eyes" just a few minutes before. Or however long it'd been.

I followed Kelly to the hallway where Theo, Hogan, and Tina were no longer present and I grabbed her by the elbow. She didn't turn around.

"Listen," I said. "Don't feel bad."

"Hi, Mr. Walters," Kelly said. And right there in front of us was Mr. Walters: my favorite high school teacher by a long shot. I never knew his first name.

"Hi, Kelly," he said, looking at her. And then, "Hey Jimmy. What is it she shouldn't feel bad about?"

"We just made out beneath the bleachers," I said. "And we're both married."

"Jesus Christ, Jimmy," Kelly said.

"Well," Mr. Walters said and smiled. "Isn't that something?"

Mr. Walters, my 11th-grade English teacher. More than any other living soul, he got me interested in literature and what I thought of at the time as "deep thinking." He had a way of figuring out what art form his students were interested in and translating that interest into an interest in reading. It could be rap music, television, video games—anything, really. He'd take that kernel of interest and use it.

"Well," he said. "Regardless, it's great to see you both after all these years. Maybe you both needed a little high school drama, huh?"

"Who the hell knows, Mr. Walters," I said. "I don't even know your first name, by the way."

"Ha. It's Les. Other than the adultery, how's the reunion so far?"

"Eventful," Kelly said.

Just then Theo, Hogan, and Tina walked back in from outside, laughing and howling. Tina was screaming the chorus to "Livin' on a Prayer" even though it was not the song playing in the gymnasium.

"Oh no," Kelly said, looking at them. "They're wasted."

I'd hoped Hogan hadn't succumbed to the pressure. The 11th-grade English teacher surveyed the scene.

"Listen," Les Walters said. "Walk the hallways. Talk it out. There's something happening here. But what it is ain't exactly clear." He started laughing.

"Can we actually walk the halls?" I said. "Isn't that against the rules or something?"

"You're all adults," he said. "The school is yours. Just don't light off any bottle rockets or what have you."

"Roger that," I said. "What do you think?" I said, looking at Kelly.

"Get me out of here," she said. We walked in the opposite direction of Theo, Hogan, and Tina, who still hadn't noticed us. We walked past the trophy case with the old-timey team photographs of local basketball legends and long-ago state championships. We went upstairs to where all of the classrooms were and turned left down a well-lit hallway of lockers and classroom doors.

"I was worried this would happen," Kelly said. "I can't do this."

"Worried what would happen? That we'd kiss? Kelly," I said. "Listen to me. There's nothing to worry about."

"There's everything to worry about," she said.

"Why? I'm a fucking nutcase. You want no part of my life. Trust me, this will not end your marriage."

"That's just it, Jimmy. I can't decide if that's a good thing or a bad thing. I think I want my marriage ended."

We walked past rows of lockers and I looked inside what appeared to be our 9th-grade Earth Science classroom. I couldn't quite tell.

"Stop it," I said. "You don't want your marriage to end. I don't want your marriage to end. Shit—I don't want my marriage to end, even though it's been over for a long time now."

I looked over and could see she was trying to hold back the tears. Then she started crying. I put my arm around her and gave her a quick one-armed hug while we walked.

"The thought that life could be better," she said.

"Is woven indelibly into our hearts and our brains."

"You know that song? What am I saying? Of course you do," she said. "See? My husband wouldn't know that song in a million years and I listen to Paul Simon all the time. I have for years."

"Listen," I said again. "I'm not the answer. I'm years of therapy away from being anybody's answer to anything."

"I don't know if you're the answer, either," she said. "I'm just so stuck in my life. Coming back here and remembering everything and seeing everybody has jarred something inside of me. Like, I didn't even realize how unhappy I was until this weekend."

"So leave your husband," I said. "Or don't. Either way, I don't think I'm in any position to be any kind of boyfriend or husband to you. Trust me."

"Why is it that we think that?"

"Think what? That we can't be there for somebody else?"

"That life could be better," she said. "That we deserve life to be better. The whole grass is greener thing. It's all bullshit, isn't it?"

"I don't know," I said. "But I'll say this. If my grass doesn't get greener soon I'm gonna friggin' shoot myself." I laughed. She didn't.

"Don't talk like that, Jimmy."

"Not really. It's just, I mean, it's been a hard year. The hardest. It has to get better, right?"

"Theoretically," she said. "But it won't get better on its own. This is why I'm thinking of leaving my husband. Only I probably never will because of the kids."

"But leaving your husband won't necessarily make you happier. Unless he's a huge asshole or something. You have to decide that your life is going to be better, and then start living that way. Not that I know how to do that."

We turned another corner down another well-lit hallway with posters and signs on the walls between the classrooms. There was a "Say No To Drugs!" sign with a red circle around the word "Drugs!" with a line through it. Somebody had crossed out the word "No" and wrote "YES!" in a blue ballpoint pen—a move I could've sworn happened when I went to school there, a move that has probably happened every year in between. I was still slightly stoned but still feeling lucid.

"I think I'm just focused on the wrong things," she said. "I never get any time to myself—kids this, kids that, husband this, husband that, work this, work that. It really sucks. It just wears me down. And then when I do get a free minute I waste all of my time reading celebrity gossip on my phone and texting with my mommy friends who I don't even like."

"Maybe we're not supposed to be happy. Maybe there's no such thing."

"Oh, I think there is," she said. "I was happy when my kids were born. But now they drive me insane. It's sustained happiness that's impossible."

We were walking very slowly—at least half the pace of normal walking.

"They say religious people are happier than nonreligious people because they believe God has a master plan and no matter what happens, that's how God wants it to be. There's something extremely comforting in that thought. My mother's that way. I just wish I believed in God more."

"I believe in God," she said. "But it doesn't change the fact that my whole life is like one big mosquito just sucking the life out of me. The kids, the husband, the job. All of it."

"I'm not sure if I believe in God," I said, looking up at the fluorescent lights in the hallway ceiling. "It doesn't really matter all that much to me. Ever since the accident, none of that shit matters. Who gives a crap if there's a God when you're all alone?"

"You're not alone, Jimmy. I'm sure you have tons of friends who love you, and even if your wife is done with you, there'll always be a woman out there who'll want to be with you. Five minutes ago I thought it was me."

"Okay. Sounds like you don't anymore. That's progress."

She laughed. She wasn't crying anymore.

"You know," I said. "Once my kids died I realized that I had been thinking about all the wrong things. Like you said about the celebrity gossip you read. It wasn't that for me but I was really hung up on climbing the corporate ladder. All the petty political bullshit in my office seemed like a huge deal. I was also really interested in politics. Like Obama and stuff. I would read dozens of articles practically every day. I would completely inundate myself with information. I hated the Tea Party. I loved Obama. I got really hung up on the day-to-day fighting in Washington and at work I was really hung up on who was meeting with whom and what it all meant. I spent almost all of my brainpower thinking about these things. And then after the accident I realized none of it mattered. I wish I'd been more present in my daily life when they were still alive. That's really the trick, I guess. Being present."

"I don't know. Maybe."

"I don't know either," I said.

We walked in silence for a few moments.

"I guess the issue is," she said, "that nothing's going to just fall into our laps and make our lives better. Only we can make it better for ourselves."

"You mean, like suddenly learning that four million dollars will be transferred into your checking account next week?"

"Exactly," she said. "That kind of thing is never gonna happen."

"It happened to me," I said. "Today, in fact. My lawyer won a huge settlement from the driver's insurance company. Four million dollars will be transferred into my checking account next week."

"Oh my gosh, Jimmy! That's amazing!"

"You'd think so," I said. "But I'm receiving it because my kids were killed in a car accident. I lost my wife. I have no family but I have that money. Or I guess my wife and I have it. Even though she's not really my wife anymore. I don't fuckin' know. I'm a mess."

We turned down another long corridor and the rooms were suddenly all familiar to me. That one was my 11th-grade history classroom, that one was 11th-grade English, Les Walters' classroom. I hadn't thought about Thomas Jefferson High School in years, but it was all coming back to me as we walked the halls.

"Four million dollars," she said. "Oh my gosh." She looked away, probably wondering what it'd be like to have that kind of money.

"Don't get me wrong," I said. "It's obviously incredible, life-changing news. I'm not saying it's not a good thing. It's amazing. I mean, I may never have to work again. But then I'm instantly confused about how I'll spend my days. It's great, but it won't solve my problems."

"Well," she said. "Only you can do that. But that kind of money must be a huge relief. I can only imagine how great that would feel. My husband and I worry about money all the time. It's the number-one thing we fight about."

"See," I said. "Right there. At least you have a husband. At least you have somebody to fight about money with. At least you have kids who need you. I don't have any of that."

"Well trust me," she said. "The grass isn't greener at my house."

"It's not greener at mine either, even with the money."

"The grass is brown and dead at my house," she said.

"Same here," I said. "Scorched."

"Burnt," she said.

"Fried," I said.

"But now you have four million dollars to fix up that fried grass."

"True. But I know it won't make me happy. Only I can do that and, up until this weekend, I haven't been very good at it. But I will say, meeting back up with you has been a pleasant surprise. You're a pretty cool chick, Kelly Donnatelli."

"Thanks, Jimmy. You're not so bad yourself."

We walked past more classrooms and could hear the thump of the music on the floor below us. I looked over and noticed she was crying again.

"I can't leave my husband," she said. "I can't leave my kids. Shit."

I put my arm around her and we walked along while she sobbed.

Kelly and I sat down on the hallway floor with our backs up against a row of lockers. For the first time since Kelly and I started walking the halls of old Thomas Jefferson High School, we saw another couple walk past us. I didn't recognize them. Not far behind them was a pack of three girls, also not recognizable by me. Not girls—women. As they passed we could hear fragments of their conversation. "I'm just not sure if he's right for you. Just feel it out."

"I don't know, Jimmy," she said. "I guess I'm not the first housewife in history to feel trapped in her life."

"You know," I said. "Running into Mr. Walters ..."

"The old English teacher," she said.

"Right. Les. It reminded me of this book he made us read way back when. *Darkness at Noon*. I couldn't even tell you what that book is about but there's a moment near the beginning that's always stuck with me. A prisoner is pacing in his cell in, like, a figure eight, trying to simulate the feeling of walking freely. By turning in the opposite direction every time he got to the end of his cell, he could fool himself into thinking he was strolling through the woods or whatever. Kind of like a fish in a fishbowl who is totally surprised at every turn and basically thinks it's swimming in the open sea."

"What are you saying?"

"I'm saying that maybe that's how we are to some degree. Wishing we were running like antelopes out of control when in fact we're all cell-bound, simulating a free existence."

"That makes sense to me," Kelly said. "Maybe I just need to do a better job of simulating a free existence."

"I mean, what's the alternative? Actually living one? Partying all the time? Riding the rails like a hobo? We all laugh at the college buddies who never gave it up and took it too far and ended up addicts of one kind or another."

"I know a guy like that," she said.

"We all do."

"But still," she said. "Are we supposed to just accept that we're all prisoners? The guy walking in a figure eight was still a prisoner."

"I guess that depends," I said.

"On what?"

"On how we want to see it. Maybe right now is all there is. When you look at it that way, you'll never be more free than you are in this very moment. Sitting right here against these old lockers. We're as free as we choose to be."

"That's hard to do every day."

"The more the days go by for me," I said, "the more I realize I'm wasting my life. Unless I start seeing each moment as the most free I'll ever be, I'm toast."

"I guess so," she said. "We could be dead before sunrise."

We were quiet for a while, sitting with our backs to the lockers.

"In that case ... should we kiss again?"

"Why not?"

We stood up and started walking back in the direction of the stairs that led to the gymnasium. The music was thumping below our feet—"Walk This Way" by Aerosmith and Run DMC—and we walked down the stairs in silence. When we got to the bottom Mr. Walters was standing there and smiled at us. We approached him.

"Everything all settled?" he said.

"Is anything ever settled, Les?" I said.

"I take that as a no," he said. "Oh well, embrace the chaos. That's what I always say."

"We're fine," Kelly said. "I'm not going to leave my husband. At least not as of right this minute."

"Well that's good," he said.

"But the night isn't over yet," she said. "We'll see."

He laughed.

"Get in there and have a good time, will you?" He gestured toward the gym.

We walked into the gym and could see Tina and Theo slow dancing to "Time After Time." Hogan was standing by the entryway watching them as Kelly and I walked up to him.

"What's up, dude?" I said. Was he stoned? Sober? I couldn't tell.

"Just watching these two yahoos. He'd be crazy to hook up with that hot mess when he's got that beautiful waitress waiting for him at home."

"Peter Dantonio's sloppy seconds," I said.

"Gross," Kelly said.

"He won't. His standards are too high. Are you stoned?"

"What? Dude, I'm sober."

"But I saw that you went outside with Tina and Theo and they seem pretty wasted."

"Not a chance, my brother. I've been sober for five years. I'm not going to blow that at my high school reunion. How cliché would that be?"

"Good, man. I'm glad. I was worried about you."

Hogan smiled and looked back out at the dance floor. The crowd had thinned out. I didn't know what time it was and didn't bother to check.

"Should we get out of here?" I said. "Isn't there some sort of after-party somewhere?"

"At John and Katie Russo's house. In Eastwood."

"Do we even want to go?" I said.

"I want to go," Kelly said. "C'mon Jimmy. We should go."

"I'm game," I said, even though I hadn't been up until that very moment. I remembered I had to fly to San Francisco in the morning. "Fuck it."

"I'm going with the flow," Hogan said. As usual.

I walked out to the dance floor and put one hand each on Tina and Theo's shoulders.

"Let's go, kids," I said. "After-party time."

"Sounds good!" Theo said and immediately started walking toward the door, leaving Tina behind. She pushed past me and followed him. She was right behind him when Kelly grabbed Tina and stopped her.

"I need to talk to you," Kelly said. "It's important." I later learned that as Theo walked past Kelly he said something like, "Please get her away from me." Theo didn't stop walking and was heading for the exit when I got to Hogan, Kelly, and Tina in the entryway.

"So we'll see you guys there?" Hogan said. "You okay to drive?"

"I'm sober," Kelly said. "We're good." We all walked toward the exit and I gave Les Walters a wave. He smiled and waved and in that moment I suspected I'd never see him again. He'd actually had an impact on my life in his own small way and the idea that I'd never see him again struck me as overwhelmingly sad. I told the others to go ahead without me and that I'd be right there. I walked over to my 11th-grade English teacher.

"I wanted to tell you something, Mr. Walters."

"Les, please," he said.

"When I was in 11th grade you gave me a copy of *Sonny's Blues* by James Baldwin and it had a real impact on me. Reading it felt like being stoned and listening to The Grateful Dead, which was all I really cared about at the time. Well, that and sports and girls. But it really meant something to me that reading could take you to a similar state. I ended up majoring in English in college and loved it, and I think it was because of you. I just wanted to thank you for that."

"It was my pleasure, Jimmy. Getting kids to read and think more broadly in those teenage years—that's what I live for. That's why I'm still doing this after 35 years. It ain't for the money."

"You seem really happy. Come to think of it, you always have."

"I am," he said.

"Well, I just wanted you to know that in case I never see you again."

"It is indeed a possibility and I appreciate it. You gonna be okay with that Kelly business?"

"I think so, yes. Thanks for helping us out earlier. The walk really helped. So far it's the highlight of my weekend."

"Good to hear," he said.

I hugged him.

"Have a great life," I said.

"I already am," he said. "You too, okay?" He smiled.

"Yep."

I walked away, surprised by my random act of affection, but I was happy I'd done it. Maybe I should find something to dedicate my life to, I thought. I headed out to the parking lot and started the long walk to Hogan's car.

"What happened in there?" I said to Theo.

"Dude, she's seriously fucked up."

Hogan started laughing.

"What did she do? Did she say something?"

"She tried to make out with me on the dance floor. But before that she was crying on my shoulder and talking about how horrible her life is. All this stuff about her boring husband and her horrible kids. I don't know. She's a mess."

"Plus she's wasted," Hogan said. "And she banged Peter Dantonio at the Hill last night. In the woods, up against a tree."

"Oh man," Theo said. "Figures. Sad."

We drove on with the windows down and the Impala's moon roof open. The nighttime spring breeze was refreshing and Hogan turned on the stereo.

"So what happened with you and Kelly?" Hogan said. "We came back in and I saw you guys going upstairs."

"We made out behind the bleachers, just like in 9th grade."

"No way," Hogan said. They were both laughing.

"Then she freaked out about her marriage and her kids so we went for a walk upstairs to talk things out."

They were still laughing. "So, how'd that go?" Hogan said.

"We made out again."

"Aaaah!" Theo said, laughing. "That's so funny. That's so high school."

"Tell me about it," I said. "And now we're headed for an after-party with a little Kelly drama brewing with me and some Tina drama brewing with you. This night couldn't be more high school if we were actually still in high school. I kind of love it."

"Me too," Hogan said.

"I'm not nearly stoned enough to handle this party," Theo said.

"Jesus. You're a machine," I said. "I guess you always were, huh? This night really is just like high school."

We drove on while Theo lit a half-smoked joint, winding our way through the neighborhood streets of Eastwood, just like we did in high school.

We pulled up to a small, decidedly middle-class two-story house, much like Kelly's old house where I'd lost my virginity all those years ago and about the same size as the house I grew up in. The block was lined with parked cars so we parked two streets away, walked back to the house, and entered the front door. Unrecognizable (to me) rap music was playing and my former high school classmates were standing around talking and drinking out of red plastic cups. No sign of Kelly and Tina. We made our way into the kitchen where my three former high school lacrosse buddies were standing around a keg. Sean and Michael O'Brien, the twins, and Z, our former goalie.

"Jimmy! What's up, man?" Sean said. "Let me pour you a beer."

"Thanks, Sean."

The crowd fell silent for a few beats before Kelly and Tina entered the kitchen. I set my beer down, grabbed two cups from the stack on the counter, and began pouring.

"Here you go," I said.

"What service!" Kelly said and smiled.

"Can we chat for a minute?"

"Sure," she said. She turned around and started walking out of the kitchen, back toward the front door. I grabbed my beer from the counter and followed.

"No more hanky-panky," Theo said, and all of the guys around the keg started laughing.

"Tina," I said. "Theo was just saying how much he enjoyed dancing with you. I think he wants to talk to you in private."

I could hear Hogan laughing as I left the kitchen.

Kelly and I walked outside and sat on the concrete steps in front of John and Katie Russo's Eastwood home. She sipped her beer. I put mine down on the step next to me.

"It's been great reconnecting with you, Kelly."

"You too, Jimmy." She laughed.

"What?"

"It's just so ridiculous. You and me, this night. All these years."

"I know. That's why I wanted to break away and chat some more. I'm going to San Francisco tomorrow to talk with my wife about the money."

"That's good. You need to. You probably need some closure with her."

"I guess so. An hour ago I was thinking maybe I should be with you. But I'm still too confused to do anything one way or the other. Plus, you have kids."

"I thought the same thing. I could imagine a life with you in it. But you're not in a good place and I'm probably not thinking clearly either." She looked away and took another sip from her red plastic cup.

"I just wanted to be straight with you. I've got to go to San Francisco and figure out what's left of my old life and try and find a way to move forward."

"Are you going back to New York?"

"I don't know. Maybe I'll stay in California. I could live anywhere at this point. Paris. Syracuse."

"Ha," she said.

"I just wanted to let you know I enjoyed hanging with you this weekend. I've got to get home."

"So, that's it, huh? Well. You're probably right."

I nodded and looked at the ground. "I'm so fucked up."

"No, you're not," she said. She put her arm around my shoulder. "You're healing. Healing and dealing."

"Ha," I said. "That should be the name of my autobiography."

She laughed.

"You are a cool chick, Kelly Donnatelli. The girl with the rhyming name. I think you need to go back to Ithaca and make things right with your husband. I'll bet you used to be as cool to him as you are to me right now."

"I've been a shit lately and he knows it. That's why he warned me about hooking up with you this weekend. He knows things are rocky."

"Well, he doesn't need to know about a little nostalgic make-out session or two. Overall we were pretty tame in the cheating department. What happens in Syracuse … and all that."

"Yeah," she said. "We'll keep that between you, me, and the bleachers."

"And Les Walters."

"Done."

We stood up and hugged. Even in that moment I thought of abandoning the high ground and asking her to shack up in a room at the historic Hotel Syracuse to have nostalgic sex until my flight the next morning. We separated and I went back into the party and braved the 1992 class of Thomas Jefferson High School one last time and I found Hogan and we went home.

Part III
Sunday & Thereafter

CHAPTER 16

The next morning I woke up thinking about New York and if I'd go back. New York was now in my past and maybe it needed to stay there. Not sure.

New York had done a lot for me in that year after the tragedy, but my relationship with it was complex. At first New York was a blur. I'd be riding in a cab and suddenly pass a massive Home Depot. They have Home Depots in New York? Then I'd be surprised when I recognized something. Trader Joe's on 6th Ave. I remember that Trader Joe's. Now I know where Trader Joe's is. Bryant Park near my office. Buvette in the West Village near my apartment. Eventually, New York came into focus. Buvette became my daily ritual. Three types of olives, cornichons, and peppers in mason jars on a marble countertop. Jazz music. Tastefully rumpled white shirts on the waiters and cooks. Black bras barely visible under the white shirts on the waitresses. Brick walls with wine bottles lined up on exposed shelves and a stunning silver ceiling with exquisite detail inlaid.

The West Village in New York was my sanctuary. I was alone and had no interest in women beyond the odd moment of eye contact with a stranger. I rarely spoke to the beautiful women of the West Village and certainly never joined one of those dating apps. Instead I braved it alone. I saw a lot of live music by myself. When all of my favorite bands came through town, I went. I found a jazz club I liked where I could get slowly buzzed and let my mind drift. The less I thought about my life, the better I felt. I wanted to be dead while still alive. I wanted to forget everything that had happened, dull it until it formed a rounded edge. Block it out. Blocking it out was my only real option in New York.

So I drank. I walked. I worked and watched TV and listened to music and devoured the city, pretty much just like anybody else although I took no time to meet new friends or get drinks with coworkers and didn't even contact old high school and college friends who lived in New York. Fortunately, I never ran into anyone either.

But loneliness can be all-encompassing once it takes hold, and the only way through, as far as I could tell, was to reconnect with people, to become part of the human race again. That's why I decided to go back to Syracuse for the reunion. It was time to start the process of rejoining society, of getting outside the world inside my head. I had to do something.

And now, Sunday morning after the reunion, after firing lacrosse balls at a goal under the stars, after eating after-hours Peppinos pizza, after lying on the red clay tennis courts looking up at the stars, after making out with the surprisingly cool girl with the rhyming name, I was ready to not be lonely anymore.

CHAPTER 17

$4,000,000 is a lot of money. At that point, I really had no idea what Jenny and I should do with it. Here's what I wrote about it on my flight out to see Jenny the morning after the reunion:

$4,000,000. Holy shit. What the hell are we going to do with it? There are so many ways to think about it. Assuming a modest 7% return we could make $280,000 a year for doing nothing. Jenny and I could live on that, even in the Bay Area (though it'd be easier elsewhere). It's especially doable if we continue to have regular jobs—not an unfair assumption given that we're only 38.

We could take a quarter or even half of it and buy a house, either with cash or take out a low-interest loan for the tax write-off and pay it down from the settlement money. Then we could just work our jobs and collect, say, $140,000 a year from the $2,000,000 we still have left over. How great would that be?

Or we could give it away. We could start a fund in the boys' names. What would it do? A public awareness campaign against texting and driving? A fund to help grieving parents with free grief counseling? A legal fund to pay for lawyers to prosecute assholes like my guy? All noble and necessary endeavors, no doubt.

We could do a bit of everything—buy a house, give some of it away, and keep a little for a rainy day. There's more than enough to go around, at least to somebody like me who's never had anywhere near that kind of cash sitting in my checking account.

I feel really shitty that I'm profiting from this.

I've never truly felt financially secure. I've always wanted to but I've just never had it in me. I'm always thinking about what costs come next, always calculating what I owe versus what I make, never fully secure.

Will financial security really change anything? Won't I still worry? I don't know. I suppose so. But I suppose I'll worry a little less—it's only natural that I'll worry less. I hope so. I really want to worry less.

So now I'm rich. Big fucking deal. What if Jenny doesn't want to buy a house with me? She probably doesn't want me back at all. Do I want her back? I don't know.

I miss her.

The day before the accident, Jenny went to Napa. The day before that, we had an argument about absolutely nothing. Our long-running fight was always about which of us had it easier and which of us had it harder; both of us, of course, argued that our life was harder. It's an unwinnable argument and we had it over and over, and each time it ended neither of us was ever satisfied.

"I'm so sick of you saying you have it harder," she said. "That your privileged life is so hard. You go to work in a cushy office tower, you come home whenever you want and get to play the good dad while I'm here all day with these kids, disciplining them, cooking, cleaning, feeding them. You get to talk to adults!"

I went into my standard rebuttal that work is not exactly a great time, that talking to adults isn't all that exciting when you're talking about software, and, as it had done each and every time before, the whole argument added up to nothing.

"Well," she said, "you can take the kids this weekend. You're on your own."

"Okay. But why? Where are you going?"

"I don't know but I need a weekend to myself. I gotta get outta here."

Moments later she was on the phone with her single friend Laney making plans to go wine tasting and get pampered at a spa in Napa. At the time I didn't think too much of it. We were in the parental trenches together and she'd hit a point where she needed a break. No big deal, I thought. Thinking back on it now, yeah, fuck me for not seeing it. She was in the early phases of leaving me. Would we have made it as a couple, as a family, if the accident never happened? I'll never know but I don't think so.

We had a wonderful life; we had everything we needed. We just didn't know it.

CHAPTER 18

I drank tea on the Sunday morning flight to San Francisco and I slept. It was nice to see my parents and Hogan and Theo again. Syracuse essentially disappeared for me in my mind for decades, but being back there and catching up with all of those folks was nice. And Kelly of course. Who saw that coming? Maybe something will come of it, I thought. Who knows? It didn't matter to me then—I was just left with a great feeling about my first girlfriend. Maybe that's all it's ever supposed to be. Maybe great feelings about people in your past is the best thing you can hope for when it's all said and done. Because at some point everybody will be in your past.

I got off the flight at SFO and rented a convertible for the drive up to Marin. It was a chilly spring day in the city but, just as I remembered and often cited as one of the reasons we left the city for Marin, the clouds parted once I got past the Golden Gate Bridge and headed through "the rainbow tunnel," which we and pretty much everybody else dubbed it, that funnels you down into Mill Valley. I noticed a new sign in front of it that said "Robin Williams Tunnel." I drove through it and out into Marin County with the top down under blue skies and a gentle Bay breeze.

I felt good until I passed the road that takes you out to Tennessee Valley where Jenny and I had taken the boys so many times. It all started coming back and I remembered why I moved to New York in the first place. Part of me wanted to turn around right then and retreat to my West Village sanctuary and to my jazz club and to Buvette, but there was business to be done, scores to settle, fates to be decided.

I pulled onto our Sycamore Park street, an idyllic tree-lined street with large homes and (mostly) tiny lawns, and into our driveway. Jenny's car was in the driveway ahead of me. I sat there for a few moments staring at it. I looked up and there was Jenny in the front door of our house. She waved.

Jenny. My Jenny. Beautiful, blonde Jenny with the face I'd woken up to every day for a decade and a half and hadn't seen in a year. Seeing her face again brought back what seemed like every emotion I'd ever felt. Stunning as ever, my stomach in knots. I sighed, pulled the keys out of the ignition, and braved the walk across the lawn to our once-upon-a-time dream home.

We hugged.

"It's good to see you," I said.

"You too."

She broke away and walked into the house toward the kitchen. "Do you want something to drink? Beer? Or your favorite? Gin and tonic?"

"Do you have any tea?"

"Sure."

I sat down at the kitchen table and looked around. The same pictures of the boys that had been on the fridge when I left were still there as was, I was surprised to see, a picture with all four of us. She had changed nothing.

"The place looks great," I said.

"Thanks."

"I don't know why I'm making small talk. How have you been coping lately, Jenny?"

"The antidepressants have been helping but I can't sleep. I'm exhausted all the time. I feel like I haven't slept in a year," she said.

"I know."

"How's your therapy going?"

"Therapy didn't work out for me. I've been self-medicating with alcohol pretty much every day. It's killing me."

"So, tea."

"Right."

As if on cue, the kettle started whistling. Jenny fixed two cups of tea and sat down at the kitchen table with me.

"Here you go," she said.

"Thanks. I've been a fucking recluse all year. No new friends. No new relationships of any kind, really."

"I was that way for a while but I've actually been trying to get out more lately. Katie and Bill have been really good about coming around and getting me out. Most of our old friends have been pretty quiet, though. It's amazing how everybody just disappeared after the funeral."

"I know. Nobody has been checking in on me, either, other than my mother. But I liked it that way. Seeing people just reminds me of the whole thing. They walk around on eggshells all the time. People don't realize how painful their attempts at politeness really are. Nobody knows how to act after something like that."

"I know. That's why Katie and Bill have been so great. They just treat me like normal and when I do talk about it they don't say 'it's gonna be alright' or other stupid shit like that."

"Because it's not. Ever."

"Nope."

We sipped our tea.

"It's really good to see you, Jenny."

"You too, Jimmy. I'm not as pissed at you as I thought I'd be."

"Because I come bearing four million dollars?"

"Maybe." She smiled. "Holy fucking shit, right?"

"Holy fucking shit," I said. "I have no idea what to do with it. I assume you want to just split it?"

"I don't know. I'm still in shock about it."

"I think I'm going to quit my job. I'll work again at some point but I'm going to take some time off and think about what I want to do next."

"I've been thinking the same thing," she said.

"Do you mind if I hang around here for a few days? I'm gonna stay at the Casa Madrona in Sausalito."

"You can stay here, if you want. In the guest bedroom."

"No, I'm good."

"It's still your house too and you are still my husband, you know. But why do you want to be here?"

"I don't know. I just need some time to think and it feels really good to be back in Marin. I think I'm done with New York."

"I thought you loved it there."

"I did. I do. It's just I think it was more of a place I could disappear, and I don't want to be disappeared anymore. I want to move forward. Somehow I think that means I need to be back here where I feel most at home."

"Makes sense."

"You know, this weekend in Syracuse was really interesting. Those people really do feel a sense of home there—it kept popping up for me all weekend. Theo is going to start a restaurant. He could do it anywhere but he wants to be home."

"That's cool," she said.

"It made me realize I need to find a place to call home too if I'm going to move on."

"Well, Marin has always felt like home for me, at least since we first moved to Sausalito way back when."

"I know, me too."

"To home," she said and raised her teacup to cheers me.

"To home."

After tea I went to Safeway and got dinner stuff for a beef stew. Garlic, onions, carrots, and celery—all of those aromatic vegetables that baseline the best comfort foods. I went back to our house (Jenny's house?) and quietly went about the business of making dinner while Jenny sat at the kitchen table messing around on the Internet.

"What are you looking at?"

"I'm researching what to do with the money. This one guy says to just invest it in mutual funds and let it grow but some other guy says to invest in emerging economies through micro-loans. What are micro-loans?"

"I don't think your answer is out there, Jenny."

She closed the laptop. "I don't know what the hell to do. What do you want to do?"

"Nothing, for now. Have dinner. Watch TV."

"That's your plan?"

"My plan is to sit on it until the right idea emerges. Or the right ideas. One thing I learned in New York this past year is that being quiet and doing nothing can sometimes get you somewhere. It got me here."

She looked at me. I was smiling. And suddenly she started crying.

"What? What did I say?"

She got up from the table and hustled out of the kitchen.

"What?" I said again.

"This just happens, Jimmy," she called from the living room. "I need to be alone."

So I left her alone. About an hour later the stew was ready and I went to find her. Her bedroom door was closed and I could hear her crying in the bedroom. From the hallway I said, "Dinner's ready. No rush."

She came into the kitchen wiping her eyes with a tissue.

"I'm sorry," she said.

"There's nothing to be sorry about, honey."

"It's just, seeing you back here making dinner, just like you always used to, calling me 'honey.' I don't know if I can handle it."

"I know, I'm sorry. I guess I just sort of showed up once I heard about the settlement. I can go."

"No, no. I don't want you to go. But having you here means I have to face reality. I've put it off for too long."

"You don't have to face reality. You already are. This is reality. There's nothing more to face. It's just a day-to-day kind of deal. There's nothing more we can do. I figured this out this weekend in Syracuse."

"How can you say that? We can't live with the weight of this thing for the rest of our lives. At least I can't. I'll kill myself. I almost did."

"So did I. But we have no choice. We have to live with the weight. Living with it is our only option. That's where I'm at, anyway."

She started crying again. "I can't, Jimmy. I can't!"

I walked over and hugged her.

"You can. And you will. We both will. And now that I'm here and I've seen you again, I think I need to stay. We're the only people on the whole fucking planet who get it. The only way we're going to get by is to do it together."

She sat down at the table and put her head in her hands. She didn't say anything. I got out the bowls and filled them with the stew and put them on the table between the silverware I'd laid out.

"Thanks," she said.

I sat down. We ate for a while.

"You know," she said, "I used to think I knew everything."

"Tell me about it," I said. "You thought you knew everything."

She laughed. "Stop. I'm talking about way back when. Maybe back before we even started dating, when I was like 21 and graduating from college and feeling like I could do anything I wanted in life."

"'A woman of the '90s,' you used to call it."

"Exactly. Back then, everything seemed so simple. Or more controllable, anyway. I could move to San Francisco with no job and no plan and no money because I figured I'd just figure it out. And you know what? I did figure it out. I found you and, don't deny it, you were the same way. It's like we had no doubts about who we were and what was possible. I think that's why we got together."

"We got together because you had great tits. Still do from what I can tell."

"Stop! I'm serious! Do you know what I mean?"

"Of course," I said. "That was one of the best periods in my life. I've thought about it constantly this past year. I've actually been thinking about all of the best periods of my life and, now that you mention it, what made them so great was that feeling you're talking about. Independence. Confidence. Insane amounts of optimism. It's like you knew life was just going to get better and better."

"Right," she said. "And now that confidence that things will always get better is gone and I can't imagine it ever coming back."

"I know. That's how it feels. But it has to come back, right?"

"I certainly hope so," she said. She took another bite of her stew. "I need wine," she said and got up from the table and went to the kitchen counter and grabbed a three-quarter-filled bottle of wine. "Do you want any?"

"No. Well, yes. But no, you know?"

She filled up two glasses and put them on the table. "Just drink it, dummy."

"You're the best," I said. "Well maybe there's a new way to

think about it. Maybe there's something beyond that feeling we're talking about. Like, knowing that the world isn't yours for the taking anymore. Knowing that shit happens. That really, really, really bad shit happens. We know that now and that old childlike way of believing it'll all work out without bad shit happening is gone. Maybe there's a way to believe that things will all work out in spite of the fact that bad shit happens. Maybe, in fact, knowing that bad shit has happened and will continue to happen makes believing life will get better more believable."

She paused. "So, no pain, no gain? Is that what you're saying?"

"Well, I thought I was coming up with something a little more brilliantly philosophical than that but yeah, that's basically what I'm saying."

"Maybe," she said.

"I mean, we have to make a choice. We can wallow in this shit for the rest of our lives if we want, in which case we really should just kill ourselves because what's the point of that? Or we can accept that this pain is always going to be there and go out and find something to hope for."

"Like what?" she said.

"I have no idea. But something. Maybe we hope to find a way to move forward. Maybe that's all we can hope for. Maybe we just hope to get some semblance of our lives back together and simply move forward."

"One day at a time. One foot in front of the other, right?"

I laughed. "Look, I realize my analysis doesn't go beyond coffee-cup slogans, but maybe coffee-cup slogans and bumper stickers actually hold the secrets of life."

She laughed.

"I'm only half-kidding," I said.

"Maybe," she said again and took another sip of her wine.

"I think I need to stay here for a while and figure out how to do that."

"I think you do too."

"Really?"

"I can't even begin to think about you and our future but I can think about you staying here for a while. I haven't been able to just sit and talk like this all year. You need to stay."

"Okay."

"But I don't want to talk too much, you know? I know that sounds crazy but I don't want to analyze everything all the time, okay?"

"Okay."

"Thank you. Just stay."

"Okay. I'll stay."

For the next three days I stayed in the guest bedroom, lying low. On the first day back in Mill Valley I went to the coffee shop in town and drank coffee and read the papers and checked in on work. On the second day back in Mill Valley I resigned from my job via e-mail. My boss wished me luck via e-mail, said he understood (I told him I was working through some personal issues—didn't mention the settlement), and he offered to be a recommendation for future jobs. He was (is) a good guy.

In the afternoons I putzed around the house and made dinner, usually something fairly elaborate—cooking was a huge creative outlet for me before the boys died and it was coming back, meal by meal, after a year in New York of eating almost every meal out at places like Buvette. Jenny and I didn't eat at the dinner table the way we had that first night but instead ate in front of the television, binge-watching shows we'd each lost touch with in the last year. *Breaking Bad. Mad Men. Game of Thrones.* We watched a lot of old Bill Murray movies. Chevy Chase movies. We didn't say much; we just ate and watched and settled in.

Jenny was still going into her job in the city during the day. After she left during those first three days back in Mill Valley, I went into Charlie and Teddy's rooms after coming home from the coffee shop. Teddy's still had his crib in it, and it still had Jenny's old framed poster on the wall with oversized block letters that read "YOU ARE SO LOVED!" and there was a dresser that doubled as a changing table where diapers and wipes were still fully stocked. The dresser was still full of Teddy's toddler clothes. Charlie's room was much the same with a bunk bed for future slumber parties and another full dresser and a full closet. I would sit in each and picture them running in and out in their pajamas, both boys freshly clean after bath time, forever frozen at ages two and four.

On day three I was sitting on Charlie's floor and noticed a collection of toys beneath his bed. Connect Four. A children's Polaroid camera. A sticker book. I crawled under the bed to grab the toys and noticed a Polaroid hidden beneath the mattress and the bed frame. I pulled it out and crawled out from under the bed. A picture of me and Jenny on the kitchen floor, crawling toward him, pretending we were zombies. It was a poorly-taken picture—off center, cropped, a little fuzzy—but he'd taken it himself and he must've liked it and hidden it beneath his bed where only he knew about it, hiding something being the kind of thing a little boy at the age of four would've just learned to think was cool, even if that something was a poorly-taken picture of your parents.

When Jenny got home from work I told her about it and showed her the picture and she burst into tears. We hugged and cried for a while. I don't know for how long.

On the morning of the fourth day I received confirmation that the money had been deposited in my checking account and was cleared for use. I logged into my account just to see the ridiculously large number of zeros. And for the next two months after that we did nothing with it. We did nothing at all, really. Jenny quit her job and spent most days shopping around at estate sales, walking through dead people's homes looking for unique furniture and art. She said there was something about walking through those homes that was calming. She would imagine what their lives were like, how they came to acquire all of this stuff. She escaped.

I went to a place called Cibo in Sausalito every day and had breakfast, much like my mornings at Buvette in the Village. I began writing there, at first just some dumb stories I made up, but over time it became an autobiographical journal (eventually this very memoir). It was a diary of my feelings; how I got from the distant-seeming past to then and there in that coffee shop. It was helpful.

But we still had the issue of what to do with the money and we still had the issue of what to do with each other. About two months after I came home to Mill Valley, Jenny and I were drinking wine and watching TV and, out of nowhere, we made love on the couch. Afterwards, we got dressed again and muted the TV and talked in the late-night glow of the TV light.

"Well," I said. "Wow."

"I miss you. I want you back."

"Wow," I said again. "I want you back too. We need each other."

"But it's more than that. I can't just walk away from our history. We've been through everything together. This past year alone has been hell."

"Same here. It's why I can't go back to New York. Maybe ever. I, like, disappeared from the face of the earth and I was miserable the entire time."

"Same here," she said.

"I didn't even know if I wanted to be back here with you," I said, "though I kinda thought I did. But I was just so miserable I was better off just being alone."

"I thought about you all the time but I couldn't bring myself to forgive you. And after a while I realized it wasn't your fault. It was just a stupid fucking accident. And there was no reason for it and nothing could've prevented it. But I guess I needed to be alone too. I don't know why I still kept you away even after I accepted that it wasn't your fault."

"I'm not sure I have ever accepted that it wasn't my fault, or if I ever will. If it wasn't my fault then it was nobody's fault, and I can't really accept that. There are a million things I could've done to prevent it. I could've not gone to the store at all, for starters."

She started crying.

"I'm sorry," I said.

"It's not your fault," she said. "It was just a stupid fucking accident."

"I meant for bringing it up."

"It's fine. We have to talk about it."

"I guess so," I said.

Nevertheless, we were quiet for a good long while after that. Jenny put her head in my lap and I sipped wine. Eventually we went to bed—in her bed, our bed—and slept in late.

The following week I came home from the coffee shop and Jenny was blasting "We Got The Beat" on the stereo and setting up two new lamps she'd found at an estate sale. They were in the shape of giant Buddhas.

"Like 'em?"

"Very nice," I said.

"Yeah, they're from this woman who used to travel the world collecting stuff. These two are from Vietnam. Cool, huh?"

"Jenny?" I said.

"Uh-oh," she said.

"No, it's a good thing. I think."

"What is it?" she said.

"I think I know what to do with the money. Or at least some of it."

"Yeah?" she said. "What?"

"It's two things, actually. One is to start a foundation to help poor kids. The other is to travel, like forever."

"Whoa, okay. Why a foundation for poor kids? I mean, I

love the idea but why?"

"Well," I said. "Just spending the money on ourselves didn't sit well with me. So I figured we should do something that involves kids. A fund for Charlie and Teddy. At first I was thinking of a fund that campaigns against texting and driving but ..."

"Yeah," she said. She sat down on the couch.

"But that's just so narrow and lame and the results would be totally immeasurable. Too intangible. Too specific. But a foundation that helps poor kids would be something we could see. It would have a real impact on real kids. I haven't figured out the details yet—like do we use existing charities to funnel the money or do we do it totally on our own—but I think it's the right thing to do. Maybe use one million of the four to get it going and use that to raise money from other folks. I figure everybody we know will contribute money to it, just because. It's something they can do for us, you know? After a year of not knowing how to act around us they'll probably jump at the chance to do something. What do you think?"

She smiled and started crying. "I love it," she said and put her head in her hands. "It's a great idea. I'm in."

"Look," I said, and sat down next to her and put my arm around her. "I felt the same way when I came up with it in the coffee shop this morning, but it leaves open the question of what to do with the rest. And that's why I think we need to travel. We used to be so adventurous when we were younger. It's how we landed in California and even how we ended up in Marin. We've got to get back to that. We've got to move forward, so I figured why not literally be on the move. Let's go to Vietnam and shop for Buddha lamps."

"I love it," she said again. "I mean, fuck it, right?"

"Right. I figure we can run the foundation online from wherever we are. Let's just put our shit in storage and go. No plan, no map. Just wherever we feel like going next. We can stop and live somewhere for a while if we like it or we could just keep moving. It'll give us something to live for. The adventure. I've always had a thing for Scandinavia."

"Why not?" she said.

The next day, Hogan called.

"What's up, my brother? How've you been?"

"I'm good, dude. What's new in the Cuse?"

"I'm going to help Theo run his restaurant. I heard you're our chief benefactor so I figured I'd let you know."

"Oh shit. There goes a good investment. Down the toilet."

"Fuck you!" Hogan said.

"I'm stoked, man. That sounds great. Is Theo's hot girl-friend still in the picture?"

"Oh yeah. Niko. She's going to be our hostess and manage the front of the house. I'm managing the waitstaff and the cleaning staff while Theo runs the kitchen. You gotta come back and see it."

"Back to Syracuse? Twice in one year? I haven't been there twice in the last decade. But yeah, I suppose I should come and actually see the toilet I'm flushing my money down."

"Dick," he said. "Seriously, though, how are things with you? Where are you?"

"I'm in California, back together with Jenny."

"Oh, wow. So good to hear, my brother. So good to hear."

"Yeah, we're good. We're going to travel the world for a while. No plans beyond that."

"Well make Syracuse your first stop!"

"I might, dude. I just might."

Two weeks later we put our house on the market (it sold for a fortune), put all of our stuff in storage, and bought tickets to Syracuse, then London, and nothing beyond that. We considered keeping the house since it was where we'd all lived as a family, but that ended up being the very reason we needed to sell it. In that same spirit I decided not to go back to New York. I hired a service to clear out my apartment and ship everything to our storage unit in San Rafael, and I gave notice to my landlord over e-mail. Free and clear, we packed up two huge suitcases apiece and boarded a one-way ticket to my hometown.

When I got off the plane at Hancock International Airport it felt familiar. It still felt small to me but somehow not as small as the last time when I landed from New York. There was a bustle to it that had been missing (at least to me) the last time I was here. My mother was once again waiting outside of security in her same jacket and scarf.

"There they are! The beautiful couple."

"Hi Mom," I said.

"Hi!" Jenny said and wrapped her arms around my mother. My mother hugged her and then hugged me.

"I'm so happy you two are back together. I always knew you'd get back together." Jenny rolled her eyes when my mother wasn't looking, but in fact my mother was right all along. I thought of that old Mark Twain line, "When I was a boy of fourteen, my father was so ignorant I could hardly stand to have the old man around. But when I got to be twenty-one, I was astonished at how much he had learned in seven years."

We drove back to my parents' house and I made plans to meet up with Theo and Hogan at their new restaurant. Jenny and I drove my mother's Chrysler LeBaron to Armory Square. Armory Square used to be a bad part of downtown Syracuse, populated by bums and hookers who actually walked the street. But the city had made a significant investment in the area and it was now filled with restaurants, bookstores, retail shops, and bars, all along streets with electronic parking meters and brick-lined sidewalks.

We passed by a bar called Mulrooney's.

"See that place?" I said.

"Mulrooney's?" Jenny said.

"Yeah, Mully's. Theo and I shroomed in there on a weeknight back in high school and watched Hogan play guitar at an open mic night. Back then it was a shithole where underage kids could drink with our shitty fake IDs and shroom. Now it looks nice. It has a lit-up sign and everything."

"Oh, you crazy kids," Jenny said. "I never did mushrooms until college."

"Well, we were legends, Jenny. Legends."

"Dork," she said.

We found a spot and parked and walked into Theo's new restaurant—"Pai"—and saw the exotically beautiful Niko standing behind a podium.

"You must be Niko," I said. "Table for two?"

"You must be Jimmy! Theo told me to take good care of you!"

"Great!" I said.

The atmosphere was calming. It was dark with a subtle golden glow emanating from tasteful and vaguely Asian-looking light fixtures hanging from the ceiling. There was a spicy aroma in the air—also Asian but nevertheless new to me. The place was nearly full. Niko walked us over to a booth near the kitchen with a "RESERVED" card on it and sat us down.

"No menus," Niko said. "Theo has a special plan for you." So we ordered drinks and, a few minutes later, Hogan delivered them.

"I know who the gin and tonic is for," he said. He set down Jenny's wine first and then mine.

"Hogan!" Jenny said. She got up and hugged him. "I feel like I haven't seen you since our wedding!"

"I know, crazy huh?" Hogan sat down in the booth next to me

"So how's business?" I said and put my arm around his shoulder.

"It's going great, man. Look around. It's almost full on a Tuesday night."

"Today's Tuesday?"

We laughed. "It's like this almost every night and it's packed on the weekends. We got a great review in the *Post Standard* about a week after we opened and it's been going gangbusters ever since. Theo's an insane chef. I guess he wasn't just smoking grass all those years in Thailand."

"Well," I said, "let's not get carried away."

"I know. But he makes stuff nobody's ever had before. It's like real Thai stuff. He could've opened this up anywhere and he chose here."

"So awesome, Hogan," Jenny said.

"Can't wait to try it," I said. I took a sip of my drink. "I thought this at the reunion too but it seems like there are more people in Syracuse than I remembered. I never really thought about it much—I just always assumed everybody left after the manufacturing jobs dried up. Like all the rust-belt cities. But when I was back for the reunion I realized tons of people just stayed. It's kind of bustling, actually."

"Don't sleep on Syracuse, my brother," Hogan said. "It's coming back. There are a bunch of tech companies here, actually. People are actually moving here now."

"Interesting. Can't beat the cost of living, I guess. I'm just glad to see our hundred grand didn't go to waste. At least not yet."

He laughed. "We're making it happen, Jimmy. Making it happen."

"So," Jenny said, "what's up with your love life, Hogan? Any ladies in the picture?"

"Always. There are a few. I had a girlfriend for a while but she wanted to get too serious."

"What's wrong with that?" Jenny said. "Are you too cool for marriage?"

"No, just waiting on the right girl."

"At the right age," I said. "Hogan likes a solid decade between him and his ladies."

"Oh Hogan," Jenny said. "So cliché."

"That's not true!" Hogan said.

Theo came out of the kitchen. There was a waiter trailing behind him holding a tray full of dishes.

"What's up!" Theo said. "You're back!" I got up and hugged him and introduced him to Jenny.

"I've heard a lot about you," Jenny said and stood up and hugged him. "Something about mushrooms on a school night."

"I can neither confirm nor deny," Theo said. We sat and the waiter started loading dishes onto our table. Hogan hopped up. Theo started rattling off the names in Thai and gave fast-talking descriptions of the food as the plates emanated incredible new scents. Hot peppers, basil, grains, beef, cumin, brown sugar, and garlic. Somehow the individual ingredients were perceptible by smell as he named them.

We ate while Theo and Hogan went back to work servicing the rest of their (our) guests.

"I could live here someday," Jenny said.

"What? Are you serious?"

"Yeah," she said. "It's homey. And it's almost like you're building something new here without even knowing it."

"Huh," I said. "Right here in Zerocuse."

"Don't make fun. I'm getting a vibe right now."

"A Syracuse vibe."

"I don't know. I'm liking it."

"Well," I said. "Let's let it sit for a while and see if it comes back. We're going to London. Our plane leaves tomorrow."

"I know, I know. I'm just getting a vibe. Nothing more, nothing less."

"You are unbelievable," I said.

"What?" she said.

"I just can't believe you're considering this place."

"It's just a vibe, Jimmy. Just a vibe."

I let it die and we got on with our meal, me dreaming of Scandinavia, Jenny, presumably, dreaming of Zerocuse.

After dinner we sat at the bar and nursed drinks while the final patrons filed out and Niko, Hogan, Theo, and the staff cleaned and closed the books. A mellow, jazzy electronica-type jam was playing on the stereo. There's probably a name for the genre. Eventually the waitstaff was gone and Hogan and Theo were behind the bar closing the books.

"Pai," I said. "Why'd you name this place 'Pai'? Like 'hair pie'?"

"Oh Jesus," Jenny said.

"No, dumbass. It's a town in northern Thailand in the Mae Hong Son province."

"My hung son," Hogan said.

"You guys are children," Jenny said.

"It's way up there, almost all the way up to Myanmar. I spent a year there and really learned how to cook. I picked up a pound of weed in Chiang Mai and just started wandering north until I found this tiny little town surrounded by a jungle. I met this short little dude named Joe Phuan who had a little food stand—a shack, really—where all he made were whole chickens chopped up and mixed with chili peppers and basil and fish sauce served on a cup of rice."

"His name was Joe?" I said.

"Yeah. It's actually a super common first name in Thailand. Like top-10 or -20 most popular."

"That's ridiculous."

"I know," Theo said. "But the food he was making was the best thing I'd ever had. He had his own chickens wandering around behind the shack, and he'd make a few each day and chop 'em up and sell them on the rice with the fish sauce vinaigrette. Really simple and insanely delicious. He made his own fish sauce too. At that point my Thai was decent enough so I told him I'd work for free if he taught me how to make the chicken with the chilies and the homemade fish sauce. He was cool about it and of course he liked to smoke too, so we'd just get stoned every morning and get to work on his recipe. Over and over, every day, and every day people from the village would come by and eat it for like $2 a pop. And of course he knew how to make all sorts of other northern Thai recipes, so I just decided to stay in that little town for as long as he'd let me learn from him."

"That's awesome," I said.

"Originally he wanted to name this place 'Joe,'" Hogan said. "But I wouldn't let him."

"Good choice," Jenny said. "I like 'Pai.'" And before we could get out the laugh she said, "You guys are pervs."

"Children," Niko said as she walked past.

"Joe couldn't pay me and eventually I ran out of money and had to take a cooking job at a resort," Theo said. "But that year was really the foundation of this place. It's where I got all of the ideas for the menu. The fish-sauce chicken wings are our best seller."

"I'm impressed, dude," I said. "You're really onto something original."

"And it's cool that you're doing it here," Jenny said. "In Syracuse."

"Which we're leaving tomorrow," I said.

"So you've stated," she said. "Don't you miss it here, though?"

I hesitated.

"Thinking of moving back, dude?" Hogan said. "I thought you were too big for this place. Dr. Manhattan."

"He's done with New York," Jenny said.

"It's true. She just started in on this Syracuse nonsense," I said. "I don't know where it came from. I have no intention of moving back here."

"You never know," Jenny said. "That's all I'm saying." Theo and Hogan laughed.

"Anyway," I said.

"Well," Theo said, "we're all wrapped up here. You guys want to go out?" He cleared our glasses and put them in the mini dishwasher behind the bar.

"You know what I want to do?" I said. "I want to go to the tennis club again. Center court."

"I love it," Hogan said.

Theo, Niko, Hogan, and Jenny were lying in a line beside me on the red clay tennis court looking up at the late summer midnight sky. Theo pulled a joint out of his pocket and lit it, puffed it, and passed it to Niko. Niko took a puff and reached over Hogan's chest and passed it directly to Jenny, who then passed it to me. We passed the joint in this order for a while in silence. The night air smelled like adolescence.

"Have you guys ever heard of the unified theory of everything?" Theo asked.

"No."

"No."

"No."

"Yes," Niko said. "And I bet you're about to explain it again."

"It's a single theory that explains both the infinitely vast universe and the infinitely small universe. Like, the universe of outer space is supposedly infinitely vast. We don't really know how big it is. Some say it's infinite. But we don't know how small matter is either. Like the closer you look into an atom you just see these strings of vibrating energy. It's impossible to know how small it gets. Maybe infinitely small. Like if you divide a number by another number you get a smaller number, and you could just do that to infinity."

Jenny passed me the joint and I puffed it. I wasn't afraid of being stoned anymore.

"Like, reverse infinity," I said. "Negative infinity."

"Yeah," Theo said. "So, this theory essentially combines the infinitely large and the infinitely small. At some point they connect. It reconciles the theory of relativity with string theory. Or something like that. If it's true it would explain the entire universe. It would explain how we all got here and why we exist."

"Some of us use God for that," Hogan said.

"Well, it would tell us all why we're here."

"How?" I said.

"Because it means we're all one thing. Everything is just one thing. The past, the present, the future. It's a unified theory. I may not have it exactly right, but if you believe that then you realize that we're creating our own future with every passing thought. We're creating our own past too. It explains why we ended up where we did, like, what would've happened if we'd made other choices in life."

I didn't know if anything Theo was saying was true. It didn't matter.

"Well I think about that all the time," I said. "I can't help but feel completely lucky and completely fucked, all at the same time. And I feel that way all the time, but I'm learning to live with it. Same with Jenny."

"Yep," she said. She was always quiet when she was stoned. I'd forgotten that.

"The reason we're lying here on this tennis court right now smoking this joint—which is just about gone, by the way—just like we did when we were teenagers is because we always wanted to be doing this. We're creating this moment as we speak but we also created this moment way back then. It's all the same thing."

"This is the third time I've heard you talk about this and I still don't understand it," Niko said.

"It's really simple," Theo said. "We choose to be where we are, all the time."

"Choice, man," Hogan said. "A conscious choice." He laughed to himself.

"So you're saying life is one big choice," I said. "We can choose to live or we can put our heads in the oven. There's no in-between. This whole year's been in-between for me and I'm so fucking done with in-between."

"Me too," Jenny said.

"Me three," Niko said.

"Me four," Hogan said.

"Me five," Theo said. "It's why I came home and started

Pai. I needed to choose my life. This life. Wandering around Thailand was cool but it wasn't a choice. It was an in-between, like New York for you, Jimmy. It's why I'm committing myself to this foxy babe right here."

Theo rolled over and wrapped his arms and legs around Niko, who laughed and shoved him aside and sent a gentle ripple through our line of bodies on the red clay tennis court.

"So you moving back to the Cuse, dude?" Hogan said.

"No clue, man. All I can tell you is I'm happy right now. Right in this moment."

"And that's all there is," Theo said. "That's all there will ever be."

"I'm stoned," Jenny said.

"Me too," a few of us said at the same time.

CHAPTER 19

One night in New York at about 11 o'clock I decided to walk to Brooklyn. I had been drinking at McSorley's in the East Village since sometime after work and had skipped dinner again. They served beers in these old-timey half-pint mugs with handles, two at a time. I found a spot in the corner near an old photo of JFK drinking a beer with his wayfarers on. I drank and read the *Times* cover to cover. In the days leading up to that one I hadn't been getting more than two hours of sleep in a row. I'd drink myself to sleep, wake up, lie there for a while, fall back asleep, wake up again, etc. So by the time I reached hour five at McSorley's, I needed to get out of there and sober up. I was too tired to sleep and as I stood up to leave the idea hit me: a nice long walk over the Brooklyn Bridge to clear my head. I tossed the newspaper onto the bar and snuck one of their half-pint mugs out under my coat.

I walked south toward the lower east side and over toward the Bowery. It was a Monday night, which is normally just like any other weeknight but the streets were quieter than normal. They were damp and there were small puddles here and there. Apparently it had rained while I was buried inside McSorley's. I don't know why but I was singing Lou Reed to myself as I walked. "The Day John Kennedy Died." I don't even know where Lou Reed lived in the city, but for whatever reason that part of town reminded me of him. I headed south past Canal Street toward the bridge. I turned left and headed toward the iconic New York landmark.

I ascended the wooden walkway on the bridge. Even on the bridge things were quieter than normal, though I'd never been on the bridge at that hour. I passed maybe three people in total heading toward Manhattan on the other side and there was nobody on my side of the bridge. I don't know what time it was at that point.

I was thinking about Teddy and Charlie and Jenny and the life I took for granted with them. I was thinking about the old line that "you don't know what you got till it's gone" and that it's always too late once you've learned that lesson. I didn't care about anybody anymore. Once the boys were gone, even Jenny wasn't enough. Nor were my friends, nor were my parents. I consciously tried to decipher if what I was feeling was real or if it was blinded by the depression. Would it ever pass? It'd been months. Day in and day out, always feeling the same way. The pangs. And now I was on top of a bridge.

I stopped at the top and looked at the empty beer mug I was still carrying. The East River was pitch-black below but you could hear it lapping against the base of the bridge. I threw the empty mug through the wiring on the bridge and listened for it to hit the water but never heard it land.

I once read an article in *The New Yorker* called "Jumpers"

about people who killed themselves by jumping off the Golden Gate Bridge, and I was thinking about it that night. It said that most people who commit suicide do it on impulse; it's very rarely a planned event. Things get dark and there seems to be no way out and people jump off a bridge. But what about my situation? Things had been dark for months and months and there was no letting up. There was no solution to my loneliness. This wasn't an impulsive reaction to a temporary sadness; this was my life now. There were a handful of people who would miss me—mostly my parents—but other than that people would understand. Even my parents would understand. I'd finally get some peace. The East River is as good a place to rest as any.

But I had doubts. Without God in my life, it all seemed so final. There had to be things to live for. Even if they were small things. Music. Travel. Those salty eggs with prosciutto and parmesan at Buvette. I noticed that I'd stopped crying at some point. I was processing. I was fucking exhausted. And so, for the first and only time in my life, right there on the top of the Brooklyn Bridge, I lay down on the sidewalk and went to sleep like a homeless person.

I woke up by myself around 4:30 am, stood up, and walked back toward Manhattan. When I got off the bridge, I hailed a cab and went home. And that was that.

CHAPTER 20

Hogan, Theo, Niko, Jenny, and I stood up from the red clay tennis courts, still mostly stoned, and climbed back over the fence and headed to our cars.

"Love you guys," I said.

"Love you too, my brother," Hogan said.

"Same," Theo said.

"It might be awhile before I see you guys again," I said. "I'm not sure where we're going and I don't know when we're coming back."

"That's true for all of us," Theo said. Ever the stoner philosopher. "Though there's a good chance I'll be at Pai tomorrow morning."

"You better be," Hogan said.

"So where are you guys going first?" Niko said.

"London," I said. "Right?"

"Right," Jenny said. "I've been there before but I've never been to any other parts of England. So maybe we'll head north from there. Maybe up to Scotland. I don't know."

"I want to just keep going east until we come back around to California," I said.

"Sounds amazing," Niko said. "I'm jealous."

"Yeah," I said. "But you guys are starting something amazing here. That must feel good. Starting something."

"We'll see how it goes," Hogan said. "But so far, so good."

Then this from Jenny, which I guess I knew was coming.

"Well, since we're your sole investor and you're our sole investment, we're going to need to stay close to it. Maybe we'll move here when this little adventure of ours is over."

"No fucking way," I said.

"Yes fucking way," she said. "Well, maybe fucking way. I just love it here and these guys are doing something special. And we'll have a foundation to run. I bet the rent's a lot cheaper here than in San Francisco."

"Indeed it is!" Theo said, smiling. "And you know what? Just by thinking about it you've already put it in motion in the universe. It couldn't happen otherwise."

"God help me," I said.

"He will," Hogan said.

"I didn't mean literally."

The boys were laughing as we all hugged and got into our cars and drove home.

The next day, Jenny and I took off for London.

CHAPTER 21

"Do you ever wonder what it's all about?" Jenny said.

"Which part? This cacio e pepe I just made?"

"No ..."

"This balcony? Italy?"

"The accident. The splitting up for a year. The getting back together. All of it. Maybe it's part of some master plan."

"I don't think about it that way. If that's true, God is a fucking asshole."

"But maybe not. Maybe the religious people have it exactly right. Maybe it's all part of a grand plan like your mother always says. We're here now, aren't we?"

"We're here now and Teddy and Charlie are dead," I said.

"Stop it. Why would you say that?" She looked down at her plate. She started to shut down.

"I'm sorry. It's possible," I said, "that it's all meant to be."

The waves came in below the balcony and she ate a bite of pasta looking down and I sipped some wine, looking at her.

"Listen," she said, looking up. "I really do think that. I think whatever the future holds will be even better. I know

I have no reason to be optimistic but I am. I just am. I think we may have a whole new life waiting for us out there. If we want it. I love you, Jimmy."

She smiled at me.

"I love you too. That sounds amazing."

We sat quietly for a while longer and I poured the rest of the Sancerre into our glasses and we watched the sun set over the Tyrrhenian Sea.

"To Italy," I said.

"To Italy," she said.

We clinked our glasses. The sea below smelled salty and delicious.

Later that night, after watching three consecutive episodes of Mad Men, she said, "I don't know about you but I am DTF."

"Did you seriously just say 'DTF'?"

A few more easy days went by like that and we weren't so much together as nearby, separate but equal, divisible. We came into and out of each other's view in this way and hopefully always will. We decided to stay in Italy and cope, settle in, find ourselves rather than find each other. We rented the Italian flat for three months and here we still are.

It's coming up on two years since the accident. I'm not sure if I'm in a better place, but some days are better than others and more and more there are strings of days that are generally okay. My kids are dead but I'm still here. Suicide's always an option and it pops up as a passing thought now and again, as I suspect it always will (and probably does for more of us than we care to admit), but it passes as quickly as it arrives now. What's the point?

Today I'm looking over the Tyrrhenian Sea at dawn writing this. Jenny is in the kitchen making coffee.

Maybe in the end we're all destined to live our own lives, separate. This idea of colonizing another human being and living with them until death do you part (or worse, for all eternity according to some religions) is just pure insanity. It is for me, anyway, and if I'm being honest with myself it was that way with the kids too. They weren't a part of me; they were themselves—of me but not me. They weren't mine to possess.

At the end of the day, we are all of us alone. The best we can do is trust our instincts, and if we can do that with somebody we love in close proximity most of the time, that's a deal I'm willing to take.

Isn't it so strange how precarious it all is? Before the accident I had no presence of mind, no understanding of the precariousness despite all of the carpe diem/live-for-today-for-it-could-all-be-gone-tomorrow stuff you read about in books and see in movies. I had no idea that that part of my life was coming to an end even while it was. It's so strange to be so clueless, but maybe we all are. There's no grand plan and I have nobody to help me. Nothing and nobody to tell me what is right, which way to go, or why. None of us do. All I've learned is it's ultimately a lonely one-way ticket if we don't choose to be a part of the bigger picture happening all around us, all the time.

It occurs to me now, here in Italy, far from the place I grew up, far from the place I lived for all of those years after college, and far from the place I settled after the accident, that life isn't just one thing. It's a series of episodes, held together, if at all, by our memories, which themselves are precarious and unreliable. The more I try to remember how my life used to be, the more I learn that memory itself is an ever-evolving, elusive phenomenon, impossible to pin down and correlate to real, actual events. There's some neurological explanation for this I read about somewhere—the inputs that make up consciousness come in at different moments so your brain has to assemble everything you see, feel, think, and hear from a jumble of incoming data. Remembering something exactly as it happened is impossible because it's impossible to even accurately perceive something as it's happening. Maybe that's why we always remember things the way we want to, not as they actually were. Maybe the "unified theory of everything" Theo was talking about could explain it all if only we understood it. Maybe not.

My memory of the boys is almost certainly rosier than our time together actually was, and I think Jenny understands that about our marriage. I remember the four of us eating in restaurants, flying on a plane to Kauai, hiking out to Tennessee Valley Beach in Mill Valley. But I don't often remember how tired I was all the time, how bored I was so much of the time, and how unhappy Jenny was some of the time. It's not clear to me now that our marriage would've survived. Maybe our boys would've grown up in a broken home. Maybe Jenny was right; maybe this was all for the best. I'll never know.

As for Jenny and me, we ended up in this room in Italy, cooking cacio e pepe, drinking Sancerre, and taking time for ourselves. I hope someday the feeling of loss will all just feel like a distant memory. I wish none of it ever happened, but it did and here we are. What else is there, given all that?

"Jimmy," Jenny just said.

"Yes, be right there," I just said back.

"Want to go for a swim? The sun is coming up."

"Definitely. Give me a minute to finish this."

So I guess I'll end here and go for a swim, together with Jenny, each of us alone, each of us part of something infinitely larger and infinitely smaller. We'll create new memories and reprocess old ones. Maybe the old ones will get better. Maybe not. We'll move forward, just like every other person who's ever chosen to live, just like all of us, until the clock runs out.

THE END.